BLOOD, SWEAT, & TEARS

by Angela Roquet

Blood Vice
Blood Vice
Blood and Thunder
Blood in the Water
Blood Dolls
Thicker Than Blood
Blood, Sweat, and Tears
Flesh and Blood
Out for Blood

Lana Harvey, Reapers Inc.
Graveyard Shift
Pocket Full of Posies
For the Birds
Psychopomp
Death Wish
Ghost Market
Hellfire and Brimstone
Limbo City Lights (short story collection)
The Illustrated Guide to Limbo City

Spero Heights
Blood Moon
Death at First Sight
The Midnight District

Haunted Properties: Magic and Mayhem Universe
How to Sell a Haunted House
Better Haunts and Graveyards

other titles
Crazy Ex-Ghoulfriend
Backwoods Armageddon

BLOOD, SWEAT, & TEARS

BLOOD VICE BOOK SIX

ANGELA ROQUET

VIOLENT SIREN PRESS

BLOOD, SWEAT, AND TEARS

www.angelaroquet.com

Cover Art by Rebecca Frank

Edited by Chelle Olson of Literally Addicted to Detail

ISBN: 978-1-951603-10-6

For Paul and Xavier,
who make my world go round.

Chapter One

Dante leaned over the massive canvas printer in his photography studio. The muscles in his back rippled under the fabric of his snug Henley as he adjusted some dial or another, and I almost forgot why I'd cornered him in the first place. *Almost.*

Eight months ago, I'd been announced as the adopted scion of House Lilith's new princess, making me the *duchess tempus*—whatever the hell that meant. The title felt like a clever disguise that effectively kept my head attached to my body. I hadn't realized at the time just how much the role would demand—or *not* demand, as it were.

"You need a hobby, Ms. Skye," Dante scolded me. "Something challenging that might instill a bit of patience."

I huffed and leaned my back against the work table that stretched along the opposite wall of the studio. "If eight months under Ursula's tutelage doesn't prove my patience, what will?" I folded my arms, more to keep my hands from touching any of the pricey gadgets in the room than to punctuate my mood.

For a former Civil War veteran, Dante was surprisingly tech-savvy. Definitely more tech-savvy than I was. He knew his way around high-end, digital cameras and photo-editing tablets, and he had several industrial printers that fit snuggly in the studio down the hall from his bedroom. Tripods, timers, and charging cables were neatly stacked on a corner shelf. On the far wall, beyond the fancy printers and the worktable, hung naked frames, rolls of canvas and photo paper, and an assortment of tools.

"Perhaps knitting or the cello," Dante offered as he turned to face me, snapping my focus away from his more agreeable backside.

"Knitting?" I stared at him. "*That's* what you think will curb my desire to work with Blood Vice?"

"You could make the harem donors sweaters or scarves for Midwinter," he said. "Improve your rapport with them."

"What's wrong with my rapport?" My bottom lip jutted out before I could stop it. "I thought everyone in the harem liked me."

"Of course they do." Dante sighed. "But healthy relationships require frequent care and maintenance."

"*Uuugh.*" I rolled my eyes and pushed away from the table. "You promised you'd put in a good word with my new sire."

Dante had the decency to look ashamed. "That was before I knew Ursula would be given the role."

"She's making me crazy. I swear, every lesson either dissolves into decades-stale gossip or conspiracy theories that make tinfoil hats seem credible. She's off her rocker. And all

I'm doing is wasting space," I added, throwing my hands in the air.

"What about sculpture?" Dante turned away from me again as the printer sputtered out a series of beeps.

A growl crawled up my throat as my fists balled. "Sure. I can sculpt an urn. For when I finally lose it and set myself on fire to escape this nonsense."

"Don't be so dramatic. That's Ursula's job."

"Well, that's what you get for cooping me up with her for eight months," I said. "You realize I haven't left the manor since we returned from Imbolc? Not *once*."

I wasn't exactly BFFs with the queen or the well-to-do guests who frequented her parties, but I had been disappointed when the duke announced we would be skipping the Midsummer's Eve ball in Denver so Ursula and I could have more one-on-one time to *bond*.

Dante shrugged, making the muscles in his back roll hypnotically. "You're the scion of the Princess of House Lilith. Two attempts were made on her life. It's not safe for you to be out in public. Not until we find a way to stop Kassandra."

Kassandra, the Duchess of House Lilith and Dante's sibling scion. She was a sly devil, and she had the prince wrapped around her finger. Because of my inherited blood vision, I already knew that she was behind the assassination attempt on the queen. We were also pretty sure that she was responsible for the two attacks on Ursula. Not that we had any proof.

Kassandra was careful. And patient—a virtue that I was clearly lacking. The summer had slipped by uneventfully, and the more time passed without incident, the more I wondered if this weren't just some part of her evil plan. Driving me nuts via subjection to Ursula's paranoia and mood swings.

My silence drew Dante's attention. He turned and crossed the room, closing the gap between us. The inner corners of his eyebrows hitched sympathetically as he touched my shoulder. He raked his other hand through his chocolatey curls, and I looked away as some irrational heat filled my chest and face.

"We have our best people surveilling her," he said. At my disheartened sigh, his hand slid down the swell of my shoulder, and he took another step forward. "In the meantime, if my recommended hobbies are not to your liking, perhaps we can think of something more...*pleasurable* to pass the time?"

My gaze lifted to meet his, and I struggled not to squirm away from the hunger I saw there. It was too close to my own. Though, I think what bothered me most was that I couldn't tell if his was genuine or if it was just a clever tactic to get rid of me whenever I badgered him. We'd been doing this little dance since the Midsummer's Eve cancellation when the cabin fever kicked into overdrive.

"Don't get cute with me," I said, swallowing my discomfort.

Dante blinked innocently. "You find me *cute*, Ms. Skye?"

"I find you to be a lot of things, *Your Grace*." I smirked and found the nerve to edge away from him before heading for the studio door.

"Where are you going?" he asked, a teasing note in his voice.

"To beat the snot out of your top security guard."

"Mind his face, would you, dear? We have an appointment later tonight."

I ignored him and kept walking, annoyed by the reminder that someone was getting to go on a field trip, and it wasn't me.

"Knitting," I scoffed and slammed the studio door behind me as I left.

Chapter Two

Murphy ducked my left jab, dropping perfectly to receive the uppercut I delivered with my opposite glove. His teeth made a wet clicking sound as his jaw snapped shut.

"Come on, man," he groaned, easing away from me to rub his chin. "This mug's ugly enough."

"Sorry." I gave him an apologetic frown and retreated to my corner of the ring to grab my towel.

Sparring with Murphy in the manor's gym was the closest thing I had to a hobby, and it was the only chance I got to blow off steam these days. But, lately, it just wasn't cutting it. I was too restless.

I paced my side of the ring, eyes searching for a water bottle that wasn't there. I guessed old habits die hard. I'd have to wait until I stopped by the harem to quench my thirst.

The tips of my fangs rubbed the inside of my bottom lip at the thought of blood, and then I caught sight of myself in one of the mirrored walls that lined the gym. My ponytail was askew, and the scowl I wore was severe enough to cut a deep crease across my forehead. I looked like I was ready to tear someone's throat out. No wonder the rest of the guards had split when I arrived.

I affected a less hostile expression before turning around to face Murphy again.

"So, where are you and the duke going tonight?" I asked, trying to sound casual as I wiped the sweat from the back of my neck.

Murphy snorted. "Who says we're going somewhere?"

"Dante mentioned you had a date."

"Date? It's not a—you know—" He paused to chuckle. "Nice try, slick."

"What?" I cocked my head, still hopeful I'd get the information out of him. "He said I shouldn't muck up your face too much. Why else would he need you to be pretty?"

"You're good, but not *that* good." Murphy ripped open the Velcro of his gloves and pulled them off before stuffing them down into the duffel bag hanging off the ring post in his corner. "If the duke wants to share his personal business with you, that's up to him. Not me."

"So, it's a personal outing, then? Not business?"

Murphy frowned and blew out an annoyed sigh. "Come on, Skye. I thought we were friends. Don't bust my balls."

"Sorry," I grumbled. "I guess we're done for the night?" I glanced at the clock on the gym wall behind him. We usually went for an hour longer, but I suspected my harassment had cut his patience short.

"Yup. Gotta get all gussied up for this *date*." He made a face at me, but then a soft grin tugged up the corners of his lips. "You wanna swing by the harem with me for a bite?"

I shrugged. "Sure. Why not?"

I pulled off my gloves and dropped them down into my duffel along with the towel. Then I slung the bag over my shoulder and tightened my ponytail, trying to make myself more presentable for our midnight brunch. Not that I really needed to impress any of the donors.

I was still taking my blood in a teapot, same as Ursula. Dante wasn't much of a vein tapper either. It seemed the only vamps who drank directly from the harem donors were the guards.

I'd drunk regularly from donors before—with Vin and the harem at the bat cave—neither of which had ended well. The blood pots were easier. They required less emotional investment. Though, I did sometimes miss that shared connection. Especially when I thought of the rarer, more special bond I'd forged with Roman. That hadn't ended well either.

There were lots of blood pots in my foreseeable future.

"The All Hallows' Eve ball is coming up," Murphy said as we exited the gym and made our way to the north stairwell off the foyer.

"Think we'll actually get to go to this one?" I gave him a skeptical look before taking the stairs ahead of him.

"The boss is always at the last ball of the year. He likes to check out the new recruits from Denver."

"That doesn't mean anything for Ursula or me," I said over my shoulder. "He could still keep us locked up here while he's off dancing with all the fancy-fangs."

"Is this place so bad?" Murphy asked as we reached the second floor. He jerked his chin, indicating down the upper-north wing hallway. "You got a library with about any book you can think of, a blood harem full of willing donors, a killer gym, a thousand channels to choose from, and your own DVR. And you don't even have to work for it," he added bitterly.

I glared at him. "That's the problem. I *want* to work for it."

"Well, why didn't you say so?" Murphy slugged my shoulder and turned, heading off down the hallway that circled around to the harem. "I'm sure Yosh can find some dishes that need washin' or a toilet to scrub."

I groaned and tailed after him, letting the strap of my gym bag sag into the crook of my arm. It pained me to admit it, but Murphy was right—about the countless amenities. Not the maid duties. I had everything I needed and most everything I wanted—minus the investigative police work and the freedom to come and go as I pleased.

It wasn't just boredom or the sense of not earning my keep that fueled my discontent—though those reasons ranked high on the list, too. Being a police officer—and a Blood Vice agent—had given my life direction and meaning. A glowing vision of my mother, watching proudly from a fluffy cloud in the sky in between playing fetch with Maggie, flashed in my mind.

What did she have to be proud of now? The fact that I'd watched every single episode of *Buffy the Vampire Slayer* in less than two weeks? I wondered how many scarves I could have knit in that amount of time and decided that maybe Dante's hobby suggestions weren't entirely without merit.

As I rounded the corner and entered the harem lounge, I caught Murphy and the harem manager sharing a kiss behind the long counter that sectioned off the kitchen. Yoshiko blushed when she noticed me and pulled away from Murphy.

"Jenna! Hi." She giggled nervously and reached for one of the stainless-steel pots lined up on the counter. "Would you like to try out one of our new donors? We have an Alaskan on the paleo diet, and a Spaniard on the Mediterranean."

"Surprise me," I said, unable to summon a single give-a-damn. Then I remembered Dante's comment about good rapport and managed to at least return Yoshiko's smile. "I'm sure they're both great."

"Be right back." Yoshiko gave Murphy a sneaky grin before slipping down the hallway that led to the donor rooms.

I waited for her to be out of earshot and then asked

Murphy, "How's your relationship work?" I didn't grasp how shitty the question sounded until the grin melted from his face. "I've been a vampire all of a year. I have no idea how these things work or what the rules are. Humor me."

Murphy licked his lips and eyed the hallway Yoshiko had disappeared down. He didn't whisper, but his voice dropped a few decibels. "It's not much different than how humans do it."

I snorted. "Okay, don't humor me *that* much."

"I mean, sure, there's the blood sharing, and we don't get married or make babies—but you ask me, I'd rather have a scion anyway."

"Really?" I asked.

Murphy dipped his chin. "Absolutely. I don't have to worry about some ticking biological clock. I could wait a hundred years—*more*—before deciding to create a scion. Wouldn't you rather skip over that whole diaper-changing, mouthy-teenager, growing-pains phase and start with a full deck right off the bat?" His eyebrows drew together, and then he shook his head. "I dunno. Maybe I'm just a silver-linings kinda guy."

I hummed to myself and nodded. "I can see that, I guess. But I was just curious whether or not there was a rule on the books about sleeping with harem donors." When his eyes widened, I made a face at him. "Asking for a friend."

Murphy pressed his lips together smugly. "No, the boss ain't got no rule that says Yosh and I can't knock boots. He knows about it."

Of course he did. Dante would expect to know about everything going on in his house. His calm and centered attitude was likely dependent on that control. Everything in the world beyond the manor seemed like an endless catastrophe.

My mind circled back to what Murphy had just revealed. "Would you...*could* you make Yoshiko your scion?"

He made a horrified face. "Yosh belongs to the duke's harem. Heck, she's the glue that holds his harem together. I'd never dream of asking the boss for something that big. Besides, turning a lover into a scion is a big step, requires a lot more commitment than most couples are able to manage."

"How's that?" I asked.

Murphy gaped at me, surprise pushing his eyebrows up his forehead. "I keep forgetting what a green fang you are."

"Don't be that way." I frowned at him. "It's not like I can ask Ursula these things—not unless I want a warped history lesson to go with it."

"Well, just think about it," Murphy said. "The relationship dynamic does a complete one-eighty. You go from desperately needing one another, to...suddenly, you both have needs the other can no longer meet. You've got to have a lot more going for you than a blood bond if a relationship is going to last, especially once you're both immortal."

"So, if you can't turn Yoshiko, how will that affect your relationship once you do decide to create a scion?"

He tilted his head from side to side. "Like I said, I could wait a hundred years."

"Oh. Right."

As a baby vamp, certain things hadn't fully sunk in yet. Like how everyone I knew who wasn't a vampire would eventually grow old and die. The harem donors, Mandy, my sister…

The idea hurt my heart. So, I pushed it away as Yoshiko returned with my blood pot. She arranged it on a wooden serving tray with a pair of espresso cups and an orange daisy she plucked from a bouquet on the counter.

"Would you like me to have someone deliver this to your room?" she asked.

"No," I said, taking the tray from her. "I can get it. Thank you." I gave Murphy a tight smile. "And thanks for the sparring session. Sorry about the chin."

He grunted and wrapped an arm around Yoshiko's shoulder, pulling her in close to his chest. She let him, timidly slipping her arms around his waist. The PDA seemed to make her uncomfortable, but now I knew it probably wasn't because she was worried about being caught breaking the rules.

"I'll catch you later," I said before leaving them alone and heading for the stairwell that led down to the south wing of the manor.

Dante's most recent series of sunset photos lined the hallway, printed on canvases and mounted inside decorative frames. They'd all been taken in different places, none of which were familiar to me. But the duke had been gone quite a bit over the past couple of months.

He and Murphy were both being suspiciously closed-lipped about their recent outings, and I was becoming more blatant with my nosy nagging. Boredom would do that to a person. I was curious as hell what the duke had been up to.

I balanced the wooden tray on one arm so I could push my bedroom door open with the other and clicked on the light. My bed had been made while I was out, but my drawing desk was undisturbed. Not that I'd done much drawing since filling up the first sketchpad Dante had given me. What inspiration was there to be had, cooped up in the same house for eight months?

My empty blood pot from earlier in the evening had been removed from the bedside table, leaving a clean spot for me to set down the new tray. Yoshiko's management of the blood harem included distributing household chores to the donors, as well. It eliminated the need for additional staff, and it made tax time less dicey. It reminded me a lot of the BATC's setup, which I guessed made sense. Dante's familial responsibility to House Lilith was overseeing Blood Vice.

I poured myself a cup of blood and took it out onto the terrace that stretched across the backside of the south wing. Ursula's bedroom was next to mine. Pale light glowed through the curtains covering her sliding-glass door. I walked softly to avoid being detected—I was already at max capacity for her theatrics.

Movement caught my eye, and I glanced out across the shadowy lawn. One of Dante's werewolf guards trotted along the line of evergreens that bordered the property, pausing every so often to sniff the ground. The crescent moon hung low over the treetops, casting just enough light for me to make out the shape of the wolf and the ballistics vest it wore. The beast's heavy breath rose up from the grass like smoke, fogging the crisp October air. I marveled at the sharpness of my eyesight despite not using my blood vision.

Ursula had informed me during one of our many strange sessions that my senses would improve over time. Which made me wonder about Murphy's hearing loss. He'd confessed that his right ear was almost useless due to too many flashbangs in the military as a human. I guessed it was kind of like losing a limb. Some things just didn't heal, especially if the damage had been done before becoming immortal.

I slipped back inside my room and poured a second cup of blood, taking it with me into the attached bathroom. I was badly in need of a shower. The increased sense of smell had to be my least favorite of the lot, but I counted myself lucky that I didn't have Mandy's supercharged, wolfy olfactory abilities. When she was home—which wasn't often lately—she announced whenever one of the harem donors were…*relieving* themselves. Including their identity and which toilet they were using.

Yeah, I could do without that little parlor trick.

I gulped down the blood and set the cup on the edge of the sink before stripping and climbing into the shower. Murphy's mention of the DVR earlier reminded me that I had set mine to record the season ten premiere of *Henry's Courtroom*. If I were lucky, I'd have enough time to watch it before Ursula dragged me off to the library for another of her so-called *lessons*.

Chapter Three

Anastasia van de Velde sat on the edge of Judge Henry's desk in his stuffy office, getting ready to drink what appeared to be scotch—a libation that was more than likely tea. After she'd handed a second glass to the judge, she tilted back her head, flipping her fiery curls over her shoulder.

"I deserve that new stenograph machine," she said with far more conviction than any office gadget deserved.

The actor playing the title role set down the glass he was holding so he could slap the end of his gavel against his palm. "What are you willing to do for it, Ms. van de Velde?"

"Whatever it takes." She leaned across the desk, giving the judge a better view of her cleavage. "I'll transcribe *all* your depositions."

A knock sounded at the office door, and on screen, my sister gasped a split second too soon. I paused the show and backed it up just to be sure, pressing my chin and mouth into my pillow to muffle my giggling.

Henry's Courtroom had to be the cheesiest soap on daytime television. I would know—I'd seen every episode. But cheesy or not, I was proud of my twin sister. She was a small-screen diva, an integral cast member of a long-running drama plugged as *Judge Judy* meets *Days of Our Lives*.

As soon as I hit play, my bedroom door swung open, and

I gasped at the same time Laura did.

Mandy stood out in the hall, wearing holey jeans and a hoodie. She had a backpack slung over one shoulder and grasped a luggage handle with her opposite hand. Her light brown hair was braided in pigtails, and her face was clean of makeup, making her look every bit as young as she was.

"You're watching it without me!" Her mouth fell open, and she huffed a dejected sigh. "Uh, you know you're starting that over, right?"

"I didn't know you were returning tonight," I said, pressing the rewind button on the remote. "Is Cable with you?"

Mandy shook her head and stepped inside my room, closing the door behind her. She left her bags on the floor and flopped down onto the bed beside me. "He took off as soon as the raid on Starlight Harem was over. His wife is keeping a tighter leash on him since the bleach ordeal."

A couple of months ago, Mandy had been recruited to help with a case that involved one of the Scarlett Inn's previous suppliers—a strip club called the Honey Hole. One of the girls Mandy had been enslaved with had mentioned the place, and how they sold girls off to yet another illegal brothel.

After the assignment, Allen Cable, the captain of the St. Louis wolf division of Blood Vice, had taken a bleach bath in Mandy's bathroom to wash off the smell of the strip club before going home. But, when your wife is also a wolf, the smell of bleach is just as damning as the scent of stripper.

"Did she get the stenograph machine?" Mandy asked, nodding at the television. "Wait! Don't tell me."

We'd been debating the outcome of the season nine cliffhanger for months now. I hit play, eager to learn the answer myself.

As the familiar scene replayed, I stole a sideways glance at Mandy. Her summer tan was beginning to fade, but I could still smell the sunlight and forest on her. With the fully-stocked harem, I didn't drink her blood as often as I used to, but I missed her when she was gone with the Cadaver Dogs. And I couldn't help but be a tiny bit jealous.

I looked back at the television in time to watch Anastasia van de Velde answer Henry's office door for a delivery man with a large package.

"Awww, yeah! You know what that is." Mandy jumped up from the bed as the first commercial break cut in. "I think I've got some chips in my room. BRB!"

"Take your bags with you," I called after her. She skipped back a step as she reached the door and grabbed her luggage. "Thank you," I said in a motherly sing-song.

It had taken some effort, but the duke's manor was finally starting to feel like *home*. A home where I was essentially under house arrest, but a home, nevertheless. Even though someone helped with the dusting and vacuuming and bed-making, I tried to do my part by not being a complete slob and leaving stuff lying around. And I expected the same of Mandy.

She returned with an open bag of barbeque chips and a bottle of soda, but instead of fast-forwarding through the rest of the commercials, I rolled onto my side and propped my head in one hand.

"Murphy says we're going to the All Hallows' Eve ball," I told her.

"Really? Maybe we'll see some of the wolves from the Denver unit I went camping with during training," she said around a mouthful of chips.

The familiar jingle that preluded the return of *Henry's Courtroom* sounded, and we turned to the screen to watch Laura fawn over the judge. Classic Anastasia van de Velde, seducing Henry into giving her everything a court reporter could ever want. She straddled his lap and put her tongue in his ear, cuing me to look away and cover my eyes. Laura was still my sister, and the sexy scenes were a bit…*gratuitous*.

"Ewww," Mandy commented, her gaze still glued to the screen.

"Tell me when it's over," I begged.

"Did you find out where the duke's been running off to while I was gone?" she asked before crunching down on another handful of chips, mercifully drowning out the sucking, smacking noises coming from the television.

"No, and now he's going on about how I need a hobby, like knitting or learning to play the cello," I said.

"Cello?" Mandy frowned. "You mean the oversized crotch fiddle?"

I snorted. "Well, now I definitely won't be playing it."

"Okay. It's safe to look."

"Thank goodness," I said, turning toward the screen again.

"Think Henry's figured out that Anastasia's bumpin' uglies with the bailiff yet?" Mandy whispered.

"*Shhh.*" I pressed a finger over my lips as Laura tore open the delivery box and pulled out a pair of furry handcuffs and a police hat. Her nostrils flared as she glared into the camera, while Henry simpered victoriously in the background, stroking his gavel.

"I'm gonna go with *yes.*" Mandy cackled and stuffed another handful of chips into her mouth.

The show's theme music faded in as the scene went black and the credits began to roll. In a small box above the text, a few choice snippets from the next episode played in quick succession, including one of Judge Henry angrily firing *someone,* whose identity we were supposed to tune in tomorrow to discover.

"Bet it's the bailiff!" Mandy squealed.

"Laura didn't happen to call while you were away, did she?" I asked, rolling onto my side.

I still didn't have a cell phone of my own—which seemed ridiculous. Of course, since everyone I knew outside of the vamp community was supposed to think I was dead, who could I tell Dante I needed to call? I guessed I could say it was to contact Mandy while she was on assignment with the Cadaver Dogs, but he'd probably just suggest the house line that forwarded to Belinda, his assistant.

"Nope," Mandy said. "But I read in one of the tabloids that the show was renewed for an eleventh and final season. Ratings went up since Anastasia's return, but, according to the Hollywood gossips, it was too little, too late."

I sighed. "I should check in with her soon. It's been too long."

"That reminds me. I need to charge my phone." Mandy hopped off the bed and took half a step before backtracking to gather up her chips and soda. Before she turned around to leave, a toothpaste commercial ended, and the preview for tomorrow's episode played again—the extended version.

"It's got to be the bailiff!" Mandy howled.

"I'm going with Anastasia, but only because I think she'll seduce him into changing his mind," I said. I hit the rewind button and paused on the shot of the judge's twisted face, looking for any additional clues. When I didn't spot any, I skipped ahead to the next frame. It featured Laura with her hands on her cheeks, her glossy lips making a surprised O.

"What are you children carrying on about in here?" Ursula demanded from the doorway. She wore a slouchy, gray sweater dress over black tights, a look that she didn't stray far from while in the manor. Her bright blue eyes scanned the room as if searching for a third party. Then she did a double-take at the television.

"Ah, the sister in Hollywood, I presume?"

I nodded.

Ursula folded her arms. "Well? Go on. Let's see if she's any good."

I reluctantly pressed play. It was one thing when Mandy or I ragged on my sister, but if anyone else did…*ooh, boy*. Look out.

Laura delivered a short monologue without any snide commentary from the princess. Once the next commercial began to play, I turned to Ursula, steeling myself for her worst.

"Your sister has better hair than you do," she said, coiling a finger around one of her own red curls.

I huffed. "Well, duh. She has an overpriced stylist at her beck and call."

Mandy wiped a chip crumb from her hoodie. "I guess it's lesson time?"

"You guess correctly, pup." Ursula gave her a sharp smile

that Mandy didn't return. I was just glad that the princess had stopped referring to her as my mutt. Though, Mandy seemed to like *pup* even less.

"I'm on guard duty soon anyway," Mandy said as if she were granting the princess permission to take me. It was a careful game they played, trading these mild jabs. I just hated being in the middle when they took things too far, and the princess began slinging threats that I still wasn't entirely sure she wouldn't follow through with.

"Come along, scion," Ursula said, turning around in the doorway.

Murphy suddenly appeared, cutting off Ursula's exit. He was in a nicer suit than he usually wore around the house whenever he was on duty. It made me wonder if he and the duke had already returned from their appointment or if they had yet to leave.

"Your Highness." He dipped his head in a formal bow to the princess. Then he glanced over her shoulder at me. "The boss would like to see you—Your Grace," he tacked onto the end as Ursula's fist landed on her hip.

"About what?" she demanded.

"I'm just the messenger, Your Highness," Murphy said with another small bow.

Everyone was extra careful around Ursula. Everyone except me. I was too stir-crazy to bother with formalities or to walk on egg shells any longer. And I wasn't about to pass up an opportunity to postpone whatever nutty lecture Ursula had prepared for tonight.

"I'll catch up with you in the library," I said, squeezing past her.

Ursula's nostrils flared with indignant outrage. "Don't forget that you're *my* scion, not his," she shouted at my back. I waved my hand dismissively.

"Yeah, yeah. Lucky me," I muttered under my breath.

Murphy's lips pinched together, but he waited until we were a ways down the hall before cracking a grin.

"You're welcome," he said, bumping his shoulder against mine.

Chapter Four

I expected Murphy to take me to Dante's office where the duke conducted most of his meetings. The room was situated off the foyer at the heart of the house where the hallways of both wings on the main level met. It was where he spent most of his time, as far as I could tell, and it was where I'd first met him.

Instead, Murphy led me down the hall that curled around the backside of the office where Dante's bedroom and studio were located. If we were meeting in the duke's private quarters, I had to assume it was over a serious matter.

"Did someone die?" I asked Murphy in a hushed voice as we stopped in front of the duke's double doors.

He shrugged and gave me an uncertain frown. "Wish I knew," he said, then knocked.

"Enter," Dante's muffled voice called from the other side.

Murphy pushed open one of the doors and ushered me inside. Then he closed the door behind me, remaining out in the hall.

"Ms. Skye, please, join me." Dante stood near the fireplace at the far end of the room, pouring blood from a shiny teapot into an espresso cup. He wore a navy vest over a pale dress shirt and black slacks, and his hair lay flat against his head, shiny with product. It made him look older and more intimidating. I suspected he'd left the beard stubble for the same reason.

I glanced down at my yoga pants. Murphy's suit should have tipped me off that this would be a formal affair, but honestly, I'd been too excited to ditch Ursula to think beyond making my escape.

"Are you sure I'm not overdressed?" I pursed my lips, frowning at Dante. "I mean, look at you. It's like you're not even trying."

His mouth fell open a moment before he caught the sarcasm, and then he chuckled softly. "Yes, well, I will polish my crown next time."

"You have a crown? Why didn't I get one?" I teased as I walked past the antique armoire and king-sized bed.

"I am sure Yoshiko will gladly make the voyage to Burger King in the morning."

I stopped in front of him and folded my arms, resisting the urge to smile. Mandy's return had lightened my mood, but I wasn't about to get over the house arrest anytime soon. Still, it was difficult to stay mad at Dante. He was a master of charm and distraction.

"Would you care for some blood?" he asked, offering me the cup he'd just poured. I took it but narrowed my eyes at him as I did.

"What is this about?"

Dante sighed and opened his hand, gesturing toward the pair of armchairs in front of the fireplace. He waited for me to sit down first, then joined me and poured himself a cup of blood before placing the pot on the tray.

"Dante?" I said, prompting him again. The subtle smile he often gave me when I used his first name was absent. "Did your appointment not go well tonight?"

"It was canceled," he confessed.

"Then what's this about?"

"You want to leave." The way he said it almost made me feel guilty.

"On occasion, yes." I blinked at him. "I'm not a house cat."

"Thank goodness." A shadow of a grin touched his lips, and he lifted his cup of blood for a sip.

"And taking up knitting or playing an oversized crotch fiddle won't change that," I added.

Dante's eyes bulged, and blood shot out of his nose, splattering his cheek. He coughed into his closed fist before turning his bewildered expression on me. "An *oversized* what?" he rasped.

"The cello." I bit my bottom lip to keep from laughing and snatched a napkin from the blood pot tray. Dante didn't move as I leaned forward and wiped the blood from his face.

When I finished, he set down his cup and cleared his throat.

"That was a first," he said, pressing a hand to his chest. I offered him the bloody napkin, and he accepted it, running the cloth under his nose. "How undignified."

I let my gaze slide away and took a small drink from my cup. "We'll just pretend that didn't happen."

"You want to leave," he repeated, taking my suggestion to heart. "And I am in need of assistance with a personal matter. Perhaps we can help each other to these ends."

"Personal matter?" I echoed, setting down my cup.

The line of Dante's jaw tightened, and I could tell he wasn't looking forward to sharing whatever it was he needed my help with. He licked the corner of his mouth where he'd missed a bit of blood and then cleared his throat again.

"I realize that your vampiric education is still quite rudimentary," he said, offering me a dry smile. "But surely you are aware of the Sânge Institute?"

I nodded. "Ursula mentioned it. Said they manage a bunch of harem charm schools."

"Blood finishing schools," Dante corrected me. "Please, do not refer to them as anything else during your visit tomorrow night."

"Wait—what? Where am I going?" My pulse quickened.

"I'm sending you with Murphy to Bathory House in Belleville, Illinois, to conduct a follow-up investigation."

Dante reached into the pocket of his vest and produced a satiny business card. He passed it to me. "You will be meeting with the headmistress, Lady Jusztina of House Vlad."

"House Vlad? Same house as the owner of Bleeders?" I asked, recalling my tense meeting with Radu in his suite above the club.

"I would not mention him during your visit either—" Dante sighed and turned away from me. "Perhaps this is a bad idea."

"No! It's fine." I reined in my eagerness and turned the business card over in my hand, running my thumb over the embossed outline of a swan that decorated one side. "These are all good things to know. But, um, what exactly *am* I supposed to be following up on with this Lady Jusztina?"

Dante swallowed, and his jaw flexed again. He fingered back a stray curl that had come loose from his slick hairdo. "As you know, the queen has ordered me to present her with my first scion next Imbolc."

"Ah, so that's what you've been up to," I said, finally putting the pieces together. "Scion window shopping."

"Something like that." He made an unamused noise in his throat.

"And you want me to…what? Investigate this school to make sure their scions are…kosher?" I took a stab in the dark.

Dante closed his eyes and covered his face with one hand.

"Now I *know* this is a terrible idea."

"I was a detective, not a psychic." I hitched an eyebrow at him. "If you don't like my guesses, then spit it out. What's the problem at this school?"

"The potential scion I chose from Bathory House went missing last week, along with one of her dowry donors," he said, irritation lacing his words.

Her.

He'd selected a woman to be his scion. Something in my stomach clenched.

"Could she have gotten cold feet and run off?" I suggested.

Dante scoffed. "It is not unheard of, though it is quite rare, especially for a royal prospect." He paused to rub his chin, and the inner corners of his brows curled upward. "Truthfully, I assumed the same. At least, at first. Ingrid was quite reserved when I interviewed her."

"At first?" I tapped Lady Jusztina's card on the small table between us. "What changed?"

"I selected a replacement from Renfield Academy in Chicago. He went missing before he even had a chance to name his donors-in-waiting. Then, I chose a third candidate, Audrey, from yet another school—Darkly Hall in Austin. Now, she and both of her subordinates are missing, too."

"Oh." I sucked in a tense breath. "Are we assuming that

Kassandra is behind this?"

"I am *assuming* that you can find some scrap of proof that was overlooked by the first round of agents I sent to investigate the matter," Dante said. "The Chicago field office is conducting the investigation at Renfield, and the Austin office is looking into Darkly, but Bathory House falls under St. Louis jurisdiction. I trust you still have your badge?"

"No one ever asked me to turn it in," I answered sheepishly.

"Well then, I suggest you dust it off, Agent Skye."

"Even better than a crown." A smile threatened to split my face. I was finally getting out of here for a night, and, as a bonus, it was for something worthwhile. I tried to contain my excitement. Missing virgin blood dolls were not worth celebrating until *after* they had been found. Remembering that, the line of my mouth finally cooperated and flattened respectfully.

"I won't return without your girl," I said to Dante. He shook his head, refusing the promise.

"You may have to. Otherwise, Ursula will have my fangs for earrings."

"Oh, right." I bit my bottom lip and grimaced. "Is this something she knows about?"

"No." Dante's eyes widened in horror. "And we need to keep it that way."

"Of course." I would have agreed to just about anything if it meant getting to leave the manor and helping on a case. Although, postponing Ursula's hysterics didn't require any additional convincing.

"The tailor is coming tomorrow evening," Dante said, answering my next question before I could ask. "Ursula will be tied up for several hours, picking materials and colors and designs for the All Hallows' Eve ball." His chestnut eyes bore into mine. "This is a simple, investigative assignment."

"I'll take it," I answered a little too quickly.

Dante's chin tilted up, and I fell silent. "No daring heroics. A quick peek around the premises, question the faculty and pupils, and then straight home. *Simple*," he repeated as if I were unfamiliar with the definition.

"Simple. Check." I gave him my most innocent smile. He didn't look convinced.

"Murphy will come for you at 8:00 P.M. tomorrow night."

"Perfect." I picked up my cup of blood and finished it in an excited gulp before asking one final question. "I can still bring my guns, right?"

Dante's hand covered his face again. "I'm going to regret this. I can already tell."

Chapter Five

Ursula sat on one of the cushioned benches in the library, legs folded up under her, gaze stretching for miles beyond the dark, arched window at her back. She did that often, as if in a daze, and I'd learned to let her be when it happened. To enjoy the silence while it lasted.

I sat at the oak table sprawled out in front of the princess's perch, a mirror image of the setup on the opposite side of the room—table, bench, window—all surrounded by glossy, deep blue bookcases. Dante's library was impressive. It held fewer books than the BATC library, but his collection contained more leisure reads. Not that Ursula used many of those for her lessons.

Tonight, the selection laid out on the table consisted mostly of history and etiquette books. *Vampire* etiquette. I was sure the All Hallows' Eve ball was to blame. The princess expected me to know which of the fancy vamps deserved my attention, and whom I should snub for slights made against House Lilith centuries before I was born. As the duchess tempus, it would disgrace our family if I bowed too low to the wrong people. I guessed I should have been glad I didn't have to remember what to do with a bunch of different forks.

"Are you sleeping with the duke?" Ursula asked suddenly, drawing my attention away from *Blood Earth: Elite Vampire*

Families, Domestic and Abroad.

"What? No." My face warmed as Ursula squinted at me in the reflection of the window.

"You'd like to, though. Wouldn't you?" Her calm tone was not as disarming as it might have been coming from anyone else. It was usually an omen for an outburst or meltdown.

"He's courting high-pedigree blood dolls," I stammered. "I seriously doubt he has any interest in me."

"That's not what I asked, my scion." Ursula's head turned away from the window, and her mane of red curls spilled behind her shoulder as she narrowed her eyes at me. "But I believe it's answer enough. You have too much yet to learn to bother with a complex romance. If you require sexual release, there are suitable human companions within the harem. I will inform Yoshiko to schedule an appointment with one for you tomorrow while I'm seeing to the tailor."

"Please, don't." I groaned and rested my forehead on the open book in front of me.

Being cooped up in the manor didn't leave the princess many opportunities to micromanage my life, but she took every opening she could find. She was bored too, I supposed, but I had really hoped she'd spend her spare time doing something less invasive. Like maybe one of those solo hobbies Dante had mentioned.

"I am your sire," Ursula said, the calm in her voice hitching an octave. "It is my sworn duty to see that your every need is met."

"I'm fine. Really." I closed the history book and stood to put it back on the shelf.

"Perhaps you desire someone more…durable? One of the guards, perchance?" Ursula tapped a finger on her chin. "Mr. Murphy seems particularly fond of you."

"*No*," I said, pausing at the bookcase to give her a meaningful glare.

"No?" She sounded genuinely surprised. "He is handsome and pleasant, is he not?"

"He's taken, and I'm not interested."

"Ah, not your type," she said, then one side of her mouth curled into a subtle smirk. "I believe the duke employs one or two half-sired guards, as well. Of course, we'd probably have to have you fitted for a muzzle to keep you from feeding on them and starting a war with our allied households."

A heavy weight settled in my chest and curled my shoulders forward. I turned back to the bookcase, refusing to let Ursula see how deeply she'd cut me.

Of all the princess's games, this one was my least favorite. If I lashed out at her for prodding old wounds, she'd take it as an invitation to unload the blame for Annie's death on me. Ursula's almost sibling scion turned half-sired companion, the one who had sacrificed herself before the Vampiric High Council to save Ursula from an even worse fate, would likely still be alive if I'd not tracked her and Ursula down last winter.

That it had been my job, my first assignment as a new Blood Vice agent, didn't matter to the princess. In her eyes, I'd ruined the simple life she'd built from the pieces that were left after Morgan, her sire, had been murdered. We were bound by order of the queen as sire and scion, and Ursula had sworn to do her best—but that didn't mean she had to forgive me.

Ursula sighed and pulled herself up from the bench as I returned to the table to gather up the rest of the books. I avoided her gaze until she pressed a finger to the cover of *The Social Scion*, pinning the volume to the table as I reached for it.

"If you're so worried about the duke's prospective blood bride, I suggest you take a closer look at this one," she said. "It's much more thorough than the book they taught from when I attended blood charm school."

"I'm not worried," I scoffed. My face was hot again, but I chalked it up to the secret I was keeping from her about Dante's missing candidates and my pending trip to Bathory House.

I turned away from Ursula and crossed the library, tucking books back into place on the shelves as I went. Dawn couldn't get here soon enough. When I finished and circled back to the table, the princess was gone, having left without a goodbye. I didn't take offense. Her manners had always left something to be desired. Being bumped up the food chain hadn't changed that.

I stared down at the etiquette book she'd left on the table, debating whether or not I should take it or put it back on the shelf. If Ursula found it in my room, I'd never hear the end of it. But I was betting it would prove helpful during my little field trip to Bathory House. Not to mention the upcoming ball.

I slipped into the corner of the library where the leisure books were kept and grabbed a couple of random poetry volumes to sandwich the etiquette book between. If the princess spotted me, I'd at least have a few decoys to distract her with.

Mandy was already out when I made it back to my room. She still slept in my bed whenever she wasn't off working a case with the Cadaver Dogs. It was more out of habit now than fear that someone would slit my throat while I was dead to the world. Since the attempt on Ursula's life, Dante's security team had been extra vigilant.

I stashed my books in the drawer of my night table,

brushed my teeth, and changed before crawling in beside Mandy. Dawn was still twenty minutes off, but I didn't want to be caught off guard and end up in a heap on the floor.

That had only happened once at the duke's manor, on a night when Mandy was gone. Two harem donors had found me and tucked me into bed. Which was swell of them. Of course, I would have been even more grateful if they hadn't informed Dante the next evening. I would *not* be having that conversation again.

So, I lay in bed, staring at the ceiling fan as I waited for the sun to rise. If I'd been human, I never would have been able to get to sleep. Not with the flutter of nerves that had turned my stomach into a beehive. For my mind-numbing existence at the manor these past months, the events of the night had been exhilarating.

I was finally going to get out of the house—for a few hours, at least. With a tailor coming, it was official that we were going to the queen's next party. Mandy was home, and Laura's new season had premiered on TV. But what occupied my mind most was the thought that Dante would have a scion soon. A *female* scion.

I shouldn't care. The emotion I felt didn't make sense. And after Ursula's mention of Roman, I was feeling extra depraved about all of it.

I'd watched Dante snap Roman's neck. Sure, he wasn't

dead dead. And being a vampire was something Roman had wanted for half a century. Plus, the last time we'd spoken, he'd made it pretty clear that we were over. That we should never have begun. He belonged to someone else.

He and Vanessa were in Denver now, training new Blood Vice recruits at the bat cave. And I was here, in St. Louis. Half royal scion, half prisoner.

For now.

Tomorrow night, I got to be Agent Skye again.

For the first time in months, I smiled as dawn broke.

Chapter Six

St. Louis at night was a sight for undead eyes. Everything glowed brighter than I remembered, tinting the sky with an everlasting twilight that I couldn't even bring myself to be mad about. Vampires lived for light pollution.

Traffic buzzed by all around—every bit as awful as I recalled—and throngs of people dressed in their nightclub-best waited in lines on every other corner. The excitement made my nerves thrum, and my fangs budded, pushing against the inside of my upper lip even though I'd drunk half a pot of blood before leaving the manor.

As Murphy took the Eads Bridge over the Mississippi River, I pressed my face against the passenger window to stare up at the Arch.

"You realize we're investigating a couple of missing girls, right?" Murphy said with a berating undertone. "You show up there with that big, dopey grin on your face, they ain't gonna take too warmly to us."

"This isn't my first investigation, Murph." I tried to swallow my excitement and snatched the case file tucked down between the console and my seat.

Ingrid Kelley, Dante's first pick for his scion-to-be, was twenty years old. She was an avid fan of Shakespeare and an exceptional violinist, according to her records at Bathory

House. Other details the first agents on scene gathered included her physical description, blood type, and city of birth. There was also a 5x7 photograph of an oil painting that reminded me of something I'd seen in my high school art history class. *Girl with a Pearl Earring* came to mind.

Jodie Watts, the donor-in-waiting who had gone missing with her, had a similar snapshot paperclipped to her information.

"Why isn't there a real picture of either girl in here?" I asked Murphy.

He pressed his lips together and gave me a sideways glance. "Some of the schools can be a little…eccentric. They think by restricting modern technology and pop culture, they'll produce blood dolls who are purer, unspoiled by exposure to mortal vices."

I snorted. "So, like, the vampire version of an Amish farm?"

He opened his mouth as though he might refute the comparison but then nodded slowly. "I guess that's fair."

I flipped back to the front of the file and glanced through the report summary. "You think the agents who took the first pass were right? That this is just a typical runaway situation?"

Murphy inhaled a deep breath. "I don't know about typical. Kids who go to these schools are raised knowing that they'll be shipped off to one harem or another once they're of age. Most of them are thrilled about it—only the rich vamps can afford to hire such premium donors. It's not like they'll be living in squalor. They're treated like precious commodities, and they usually only serve for twenty years or so before retiring with more than enough money to live out the rest of their days."

"Hmm." I still found the whole idea of blood finishing schools unsettling. "Do the parents understand what's going on at these *schools*?"

Murphy began to nod but then stopped short. "Well, to be fair, a lot the kids don't have parents. But some do," he quickly added, seeing the horror in my expression. "The most important thing to remember is that no one is forcing anyone to do anything they don't want to. Harem donors aren't prisoners."

"So, the ones who *do* have families have parents who are aware of what their children are being prepared for?"

"Sure. A lot of them were donors once themselves. They know what an easy, lucrative career path being a trained blood doll is."

"And if their kids refuse, they can always go back home," I said, frowning as I double-checked Ingrid's and Jodie's details again. "But what about orphans like Jodie? What happens to them if they decide they'd rather not open a vein?"

Murphy fidgeted uncomfortably. "Some of them run off.

If they don't, the younger ones are put into foster care."

"And the older ones?" Jodie was only nineteen, and if she didn't know how modern technology worked, she was going to be hard-pressed to find a job.

Murphy shrugged. "I imagine some of them get dropped off at the unemployment office or a shelter. It's their choice."

"That's terrible." I closed the file and tucked it under the console between us.

"Not all of the schools are as stuck in the Dark Ages as Bathory House," Murphy said. "Some of them even put their pupils through college—House Starling expects their potential scions to have a medical degree."

It should have perked my spirits, but I only found the mention of House Starling more depressing. It reminded me of Sonja, and by proxy, Natalie, Will, my mother—all the people I'd lost. I tried to thwart the melancholy by rolling down my window. Traffic had thinned, and so had the bright city lights. I closed my eyes, enjoying the way the wind blew my hair across my cheeks and forehead.

"Better hope no one recognizes you," Murphy grumbled. "The boss will rip me a new one."

"Chillax, would you?" I leaned back in my seat, letting the shadows conceal me.

It didn't take much investigative skill to figure out that Dante had tasked Murphy with babysitting me for the night.

Tracking down his former scioncée couldn't be *that* high on his priority list if he'd moved on to a second and then a third blood doll a whole week later. There hadn't been any exciting developments at Bathory House since the disappearing act either, so even if the girls had met some untimely end, the likelihood that we'd encounter any danger was minimal.

No daring heroics required. *Simple,* as Dante had put it.

This was just a menial task that he probably hoped would curb my nagging with regards to getting out of the house. Either way, I didn't care. I'd take it.

The city lights grew dim in the distance, and I stuck my face out the window again, breathing in the cool, fresh air while Murphy snorted at me from the driver's seat.

Bathory House looked like a convent from the street. The modest, brick and stone structure was located several miles outside the Belleville city limits, surrounded by a clean, well-kept lawn. Night had already painted dew on the grass. It glistened in the light of several decorative lampposts that lined the sidewalk.

An unremarkable vegetable garden took up most of the lot to the south, but as Murphy pulled around the circular drive, I noticed that that side of the school was covered in climbing roses. Their white petals glowed softly under the security lights anchored to the roofline.

A tall, slender woman in a gray dress greeted us as we exited the car. Her dark hair was pulled back in a bun, and though her face wasn't unattractive, the frozen expression she wore gave me pause.

"Lady Jusztina," Murphy greeted her first, bowing his head slightly. I did the same, remembering that this woman was from House Vlad, one of the oldest, most respected vampire families.

"Mr. Murphy." Lady Jusztina did not return his bow, but her head cocked as her eyes fell on me. "You must be the infamous Agent Skye of House Lilith," she said, sounding unimpressed.

"At your service." I dipped my head again, wondering if maybe she'd unintentionally forgotten to return the curtsey. When she sniffed and turned back to Murphy, I realized that wasn't the case.

"I do appreciate the duke's desire to discover what's become of his chosen scion," she said, not sounding appreciative in the least. "But since that seems unlikely, and since he has decided to take his business elsewhere, I do not understand why he's bothering to continue this investigation. The only purpose it serves at this point is to further tarnish the name of our good school."

"Lady Jusztina," Murphy said, pressing the palm of one hand over his heart. "The duke has no intention of harming your school's reputation. His only concern is for Ingrid's safety. He hasn't even issued a complaint with the Sânge Institute."

The woman bristled at the mention of the institute, and her shoulders squared. "Small mercy."

"We'd just like to ask your students and staff a few follow-up questions and take another look at Ingrid's room," I said, adopting Murphy's mild tone. "We'll be out of your hair in no time."

Lady Jusztina could be as snippy as she liked. I wouldn't sabotage the small sliver of rapport I'd developed with the duke and the trust that had earned me a get-out-of-jail-free card for the night.

While we stood there, letting the headmistress stare us down with silent scrutiny, a young man in coveralls walked around the corner of the garden with a leaf blower. He got an eyeful of us and quickly retreated around the side of the building, his chin tucked into his chest. I wondered if everyone at Bathory House was as fond of Lady Jusztina.

"Follow me," the headmistress finally said, turning on her heel and leading the way up the walk to the front door of the school.

I stayed a step behind Murphy. He'd been here once

before and was familiar with the place. Besides, it gave me a chance to take everything in—with my blood vision.

At the far edges of the campus, sparse trees gave way to thicker woods. I expected to find *some* sort of security hidden in the shadows, but there was none. Granted, the school was built like a fortress. Two rows of barred windows stretched across the top half of the building. A curtain parted in one of the frames just before I entered through the front door, and a young girl peered down at me. I paused at the threshold to stare back at her, but then she was gone.

Inside, the front hall was bordered by narrow tables topped with vases of sunflowers and white roses. The dark, glossy wood of the floor was offset by rugs and the stone walls, all brightly lit by an iron chandelier that hung to the right of a long staircase. There was a quiet luxury to the place. Nothing too flashy, but certainly nothing cheap or worn.

Lady Jusztina headed for the stairs, but before we reached them, we passed a wide doorway that opened into a formal sitting area. A dozen girls, dressed and styled in the same fashion as the headmistress, sat on couches arranged in a semicircle, each holding a stringed instrument. The youngest was maybe twelve, the oldest twentyish. They paused to look up from their sheet music and regarded me with apprehensive curiosity. I returned the favor.

"All of our girls are classically trained in the arts," Lady

Jusztina said as if reading from a brochure. Then, she tilted her chin in the air. "Do you play, Agent Skye?"

"No," I answered truthfully.

"Hmm." It wasn't a kind sound, but I ignored it as she turned and headed up the stairs. Murphy and I followed closely behind, curling around the landing halfway up.

Once we reached the second floor, the stone walls surrendered to plaster. A wide hall cut a path that ran the length of the building. Down both sides, framed paintings of sunsets and fruit still life arrangements were practically hung on top of one another. It reminded me of the way Dante's photographs were displayed throughout the manor. Déjà vu hit me a second time when I noticed a painting of a sun setting behind a line of autumn-kissed trees.

It hadn't occurred to me until just then that while I knew Ursula had attended a blood finishing school, I had no idea whether or not Dante had. Because of the Eye of Blood, I knew exactly how the princess had died. I'd had a front-row seat to her memory of it.

Dante's past, on the other hand, was a complete mystery. I knew that the prince, Alexander, was his sire. And that Dante had maybe been a Union soldier or general during the Civil War. But that was it.

Lady Jusztina turned left, and as I peered ahead of her, another woman exited through a doorway midway down the hall. She, too, wore a gray dress, but her hair was cut short and curly.

"Ms. Collet has taught French here at Bathory House for seventy-five years," Lady Jusztina said. "She is one of my half-sired heirs, and she was on watch the day Ingrid vanished."

For somewhere in the ballpark of a hundred, Ms. Collet looked amazing. I supposed still being human was more beneficial at a place like this where the students required supervision during the daylight hours, as well.

Ms. Collet inclined her head to Murphy and me. She didn't look much happier to see us than the headmistress had, but she was more careful with her tone.

"This is Ingrid's room," Ms. Collet said, opening her arm to welcome us inside.

Murphy stepped back this time, allowing me to go ahead of him. The stuffy environment seemed to be bringing out his inner chivalry. I did the polite thing and thanked him as I walked past.

Ingrid shared a room with three other girls. The beds were stacked over desks like in a college dorm, one tucked in each corner, allotting just enough wall space for the entrance, a barred window, and the closet and bathroom doors.

"Ms. Collet, would you please assist our guests and answer their questions?" Lady Jusztina said. "I have calls to return."

"Of course."

"I'll send Holly and Renee upstairs before retiring to my office."

"Thank you, Headmistress," Ms. Collet said, bowing her head deeper than she had for Murphy or me.

Murphy echoed the motion to Lady Jusztina. "We appreciate your time," he said. I nodded but refrained from expressing additional gratitude. Ursula's vampire etiquette lessons weren't entirely useless, and this was the first chance I'd had to test drive them outside of the manor.

Do not cave to anger, but neither reward insult with veneration.

I considered it a successful trial run before the All Hallows' Eve ball.

Lady Jusztina gave me one last glance before disappearing down the hall, and I turned my attention back to the room.

"Which one is Ingrid's?" I asked.

"Here." Ms. Collet pointed to the desk and bed combo along the wall beside the closet door. "And Jodie's is there," she said, nodding to the bed along the stretch of wall by the window.

I glanced over Ingrid's space first, taking in the quilted bedspread and the stack of books on her desk beneath— calculus, American history, chemistry. A violin case was propped upright in the desk chair.

"Ingrid was one of our best pupils," Ms. Collet said,

melancholy softening her words. "She seemed so excited to be chosen by the duke."

"When was the last time you saw her?" I asked as I moved on to Jodie's space. Murphy's eyes followed my movements, his focus split between the room and me.

"Late Tuesday morning. She was still asleep. Jodie, too," Ms. Collet answered. "The headmistress and two of our instructors are undead, so we keep split hours. The girls go to bed at 1:00 A.M. and wake around 10:00 A.M. I looked in on them before going downstairs to prepare brunch. When Ingrid and Jodie didn't show, and we could not find them, we immediately contacted Blood Vice and then the duke."

Jodie's bed and desk looked almost identical to Ingrid's, except for a small vase that held a pair of white roses and a familiar book of vampire poetry. I double-checked the other desks in the room but didn't see flowers on any of them.

"Did Jodie like gardening?" I asked, fingering the white petals of one rose.

"She spent a lot of time in the garden," Ms. Collet answered. "And she enjoyed helping me in the kitchen."

"Was she allowed to roam the garden without supervision?" Murphy asked.

"Of course. The girls are not prisoners." She scowled defensively. "They are free to leave at any time."

"Free to be homeless and destitute?" I lifted an eyebrow.

"We're a finishing school, not a trust fund for quitters," Ms. Collet said. "We rely on *donations* from wealthy benefactors, who hire our girls for their harems or as future scions. These young ladies work hard to attain such an honor, and any of them would have loved to be in Ingrid's shoes."

Just then, two girls entered the room. One of them I recognized as the cello player from downstairs. They were both older, so I assumed the living quarters were arranged by age group. They folded their hands behind their backs and looked down at the floor as Ms. Collet addressed them.

"Holly, Renee, these agents are here to ask more questions about Ingrid and Jodie. Will you speak with them?"

"Yes, Ms. Collet," they answered in unison. Something in the robotic way they responded told me they would say whatever they thought was least likely to displease their keepers. Maybe they could leave whenever they wanted to, but that didn't mean they had anywhere else to go.

It had been some time since I'd interrogated a suspect or witness, even longer since I'd questioned a kid. So, I approached it carefully, starting with the easy stuff.

"How long have you girls shared a room with Ingrid?"

The first girl, Holly, glanced up at me. "Almost five years. She'd been here for six months before I arrived. She chose me to be her second donor-in-waiting," she added glumly.

"And you?" I asked Renee.

"I've been in this room for two years but at the school for four," she answered.

"How long was Jodie here?"

"Ingrid and Jodie joined us at the same time," Ms. Collet said.

I looked at Jodie's desk again, sure I was missing something vital. "I don't see an instrument."

"Jodie plays bass, though not very well. It's quite large, so it remains in the music room downstairs."

"Was she as excited about the move to the duke's manor as Ingrid?" Murphy asked next.

Ms. Collet sighed and shot an uncertain glance at the two girls. "Tell them what you told me. It's all right," she added at Holly's worried expression, but it was Renee who spoke up first.

"The day before they were supposed to leave, Ingrid seemed mad at Jodie. Jodie was begging Ingrid to pick someone else to go with her."

"She wanted to stay here at Bathory House," Holly added.

"Why?" I frowned and glanced around the room, wondering what Jodie could possibly have to stay behind for. Then my eyes caught on the vase of flowers again. Was she worried that the duke wouldn't have a garden? Did she think he'd look down on her for not playing her instrument well?

No one, including Ms. Collet, seemed to have an answer

for that one. They just stared uncomfortably at the floor. Renee seemed to grow more agitated as the silence stretched. Until she seemingly couldn't take it any longer.

"Ingrid caught her talking to some boy on a cell phone," she blurted.

"Where on earth would she have gotten a cell phone?" Ms. Collet snapped. She turned her puzzled face to Murphy and me. "None of the instructors, nor the headmistress, have mobile phones. The school has two landlines, and that's it."

Ah, young love. If there were a boy in the picture, Jodie had to have met him somehow.

"Does the school have internet access?"

Ms. Collet frowned thoughtfully. "Only in Lady Jusztina's office, but she keeps the door locked when she's out, and her computer is password-protected. It's not available to the girls."

I stepped out into the hallway, trying to recreate the morning the girls disappeared in my head. "Is there another stairwell to get up to this floor besides the one near the front entrance?"

Ms. Collet nodded. "At the end of the hall. It leads down to the sunroom at the back of the house, right off the kitchen. They must have slipped right by me." She paused to shake her head. "Come. I will show you."

We followed her out of the room, and past two more

closed doors before finding the stairwell tucked around a corner at the end of the hall. It was narrower than the one at the front of the house and lit only by a pair of small, dim sconces.

Just as Ms. Collet had said, it deposited us into a sunroom. The space was crowded with potted plants, and shelves of boxed herbs were pressed up against the three glass walls. A wreath of dried roses hung from a hook on the brick interior wall.

"Jodie must have made that," Ms. Collet said with a tender smile. "She loves flowers."

"The gardener planted the crawling roses along the side of the house just for her," Renee said.

"No," Holly said. "That was the gardener's son, Wesley."

I thought of the roses on Jodie's desk again, and the book of poetry. "I saw a boy in coveralls near the garden when we arrived. Would that be Wesley?"

"Yes, Wesley Arnold," Ms. Collet confirmed. "He's been staying extra late since the girls disappeared. I think he's hoping they'll return. He and Jodie were friends. They worked together in the garden."

"Could we talk to him?" Murphy asked.

"Of course. Girls, you may return to your music lesson," Ms. Collet said to Renee and Holly before pointing Murphy and me out a door that led to the garden.

"We should check in with the boss," Murphy whispered over my shoulder as we stepped back out into the night.

He gave me a curious look that crossed somewhere between cautious hesitation and excitement over the new development. I wasn't sure which he wanted more: to solve the mystery or keep me perfectly clear of any potential disasters that could land him in hot water with the duke.

I shrugged. "Why don't we wait until we have something useful to tell him."

Chapter Seven

Certain things that would have struck me as odd when I was human, I now quickly dismissed as a vampire. Parents turning their young daughters over to be groomed into fancy blood donors. Music lessons after 9:00 P.M. Gardeners roaming around after nightfall.

A large carriage house rested behind the school. The dirt drive that led up to it was mostly overgrown with grass, but an old, tired pickup was parked in it. A leaf blower rested on top of the open tailgate, and several black bags were piled up in the bed. As Ms. Collet led us toward the truck, the boy I'd seen earlier appeared, wrestling a bag of leaves as he tied off the top.

"Wesley," Ms. Collet called. His head jerked up, and for a moment, I wondered if he might bolt. "These people were sent by the duke. They'd like to have a word with you."

"I'm... I'm not finished with my work yet," he said slowly, eyes darting to Murphy and then down at his feet.

"This shouldn't take long," I said, offering him a small smile. "We understand you were close with Jodie—?"

"I wasn't here the day she and Ingrid disappeared." He blushed, having realized he'd cut me off, and bowed his head again. "Sorry, ma'am. I wish I could be more help."

"Do you?" Murphy asked.

"W-what?" Wesley tugged nervously at the cuffs of his flannel shirt.

"Wish you could be more help?" Murphy clarified. "Because everyone we've talked to seems to think you cared for this girl, but something tells me you're not being as helpful as you could be. Why is that?"

"I am," he insisted. "I swear, *if* they ran off, they didn't tell me where they were going."

"Why do you say if?" I asked, eyeballing the lawn around the school for any signs of a struggle. "You don't think they left willingly?"

Wesley eyed Ms. Collet, but she seemed uninterested, as though she'd already heard everything he had to say about the girls. He sighed and rubbed his forehead with the back of one hand. "Look, if Jodie had called and asked me to drive her to the coast of California, I would have dropped everything and done just that. She knew it, too."

"Speaking of phone calls…" I said, noting the way his face blanched and his eyes dilated. "Any idea how Jodie got her hands on a cell phone?"

"I…I sometimes let her use mine." His eyes dropped to the ground again.

"Wesley!" Ms. Collet gasped. I supposed she didn't know everything. "Why?"

"So we could talk when I wasn't here. I'd call her from

my house line."

"That is unacceptable behavior," Ms. Collet scolded Wesley. "I will have to report this to the headmistress at once."

"Where's your cell phone now?" Murphy asked before Ms. Collet scared him into clamming up.

"Jodie had it when she disappeared," the boy confessed. "I've called it a hundred times, but she never answers, and it goes straight to my voicemail. Either the battery's dead, or she turned it off."

"A lot of good that'll do us now." Murphy sighed and shook his head at the boy.

"Did you use any GPS or map apps on your phone?" I asked, trying to salvage the stale lead.

Wesley shrugged. "Sure, sometimes."

I held out my hand to Murphy. "I need your phone." He didn't argue, but he didn't seem happy about turning over his lifeline to the duke either. I immediately handed it to Wesley. "Log in to your maps account."

He hesitantly took the phone, as though he might refuse, but then Murphy cleared his throat, and Wesley set to work punching in his information. "What will happen to Jodie if you find her?" the boy asked as he turned the device back over to me.

"I'll buy her a phone charger and tell her to check in," I

said, meaning it. "We weren't sent here to drag her back to the school or to the duke. Our only job is to confirm her safety."

I clicked on the app's menu and scrolled through it until I found the history tracker. The phone had been active until around 10:30 A.M. on Tuesday, not long after it had been discovered that the girls were missing. I saved the last known coordinates to Murphy's phone so we could plug them into the car's more precise GPS system.

"Whoa," Wesley said, glancing over the top of the phone. "What is all *that?*"

"A timeline map."

"It tracks *everywhere?* Even when the app's not being used?"

I nodded. "No one reads the fine print anymore."

"Lucky for us," Murphy added under his breath.

October was new enough that the first frost hadn't yet occurred. Which meant most of the insects were still active and annoying as ever. They buzzed around my head, tickling my ears and catching in my hair as Murphy and I trudged through a soggy ravine that ran under the road leading to Bathory House.

The coordinates we'd taken from Wesley's map app had pointed us north less than half a mile, but on muddy, uneven ground in the pitch black, the trek was trying even for a pair of vampires. The first layer of fall leaves covering everything didn't help matters.

It had rained here recently, and the steep ditch fed into a nearby creek. I could hear it gurgling not far away. The beam of Murphy's flashlight bounced over the rocks and the brush ahead of us, but I didn't need illumination. I was wound too tightly, so the Eye of Blood painted everything in shades of red.

"The duke's gonna kill me," Murphy mumbled to himself for the fifth or sixth time. "We should have checked in by now, and I don't have signal down here—I only had half a bar up at the road. We need to go back and call in a search party."

"Just a little farther," I said, climbing over a fallen branch angled across the ravine. I paused to point it out to Murphy. His pants snagged as he stepped over it to join me on the other side.

"Damn it." He sighed and gave me an accusing glare. "I liked this suit, too."

As per Blood Vice protocol, I was wearing a pair of black slacks and a modest blouse under a blazer. It was the one business-casual outfit that Mandy had salvaged from my house before it was torched to snuff out my human identity.

If I were ever allowed to make an official return to Blood Vice, I'd have to do some shopping. In the meantime, I did my best not to muck up my outfit. Murphy, being built like a pro wrestler, had a harder time managing the same.

"We're almost there," I said, encouraging him on. "We can't quit when we're this close."

"If the phone was tossed, we won't find it without a good wolf. Shoulda brought Mandy along," Murphy said, glancing back toward the road.

I ignored him and hurried ahead while his back was turned, using my blood vision to navigate the rocky terrain. The creek was growing louder, and so was my determination. My nose crinkled at the organic bouquet infusing the air. Wild onion and rotting leaves. Damp earth and fish.

Decay.

"Hold up," Murphy hissed as he stumbled along behind me. "Damn it, Skye. You're gonna get me in so much trouble."

I held up a hand to shield my eyes from the glare of his flashlight as I turned around. "Do you smell that?"

Murphy paused, and we both took a long, deep breath. I didn't wait for him to reply before I moved ahead. He followed, thrashing loudly through the underbrush as he caught up to me.

A few yards farther ahead, we stopped where the ravine

met up with the creek. A trickle of muddy water pushed up over the lip of rocks that marked the end of the ditch. Just before that, in a shallow puddle, lay the broken body of Jodie Watts.

Blood stained the front of her dress. The material was torn in a few places. Some of the damage had likely been caused by her journey down the ravine, though, I imagined some of it was from whatever had landed her there in the first place. The damp material clung to her frame, and a lump near her hip revealed where Wesley's phone had finally died. An open, bloodless gash across her forehead was the most likely reason I could see why she wouldn't have answered his calls. Though, the damage to the rest of her body would have to be analyzed by the experts back at the field office before anything could be confirmed.

Jodie's pale eyes stared up at the sliver of moon, shining down between a break in the canopy of rusty leaves. Despite her mangled condition, her face looked at peace.

"Where's your friend, Miss Watts?" I asked, taking another look around.

Murphy's phone chirped loudly as if in reply, and we both jumped. I swallowed back a yelp as I turned to frown at him.

"Two bars," he commented, jiggling the phone. "Whadayaknow?" Then he looked down at the screen and swallowed. "And six missed calls. All from the duke."

Chapter Eight

Dante paced back and forth in front of the fireplace in his room. His lips were parted, revealing a glimpse of his extended fangs. It was a startling sight, considering how used to his calm and collected demeanor—even in the most dire of circumstances—I'd become.

I watched him silently from an armchair, my hands in my lap, mud clinging to my shoes and the hem of my slacks. He'd already dismissed Murphy with a promise that he'd deal with him later. When I tried to follow Murphy out, I was ordered to sit, which I immediately did. I'd been sitting for some time now, waiting for the floodgates of the duke's wrath to open.

"The potential scion from Renfield was found dead in an alley," he said, breath rasping unevenly. "When I couldn't reach Mr. Murphy, I didn't know what to think. I was halfway to Belleville when he finally called."

That explained the dress shirt and slacks. Unless we were expecting fancy company, Dante favored his Henley shirts and sweats at home, sometimes jeans. I preferred the more casual look, as well. The duke paused his pacing to stare at me, dilated eyes swirling with equal parts rage and relief.

"You can't imagine the awful things that went through my mind."

"The area around Bathory House has horrible reception,"

I offered timidly. "But we were perfectly fine—"

"You found a dead girl less than a mile from the school," he snapped. "And we're no closer to discovering who is responsible." Dante ran both hands down his face and then turned his back to me. "I should not have sent you. I am sorry."

The apology deflated my ego even more than I expected a lecture would have.

"Hey, I trained for this—as a human *and* as a vampire," I reminded him.

"Then you should understand, especially as a member of House Lilith, how much danger you are in until the killer is found. As it stands, we have no leads."

"Give the coroner a chance," I said. "Maybe he'll turn up some helpful evidence for us."

"For the Blood Vice agents who were initially assigned to this case," Dante amended. "Now that this is a confirmed murder investigation, you cannot be involved. Ursula will not allow it."

"Right." *So much for getting out of the manor.* I sighed and pressed my lips together. "I guess I'd better change before the princess's lesson *du nuit.*"

"*De la nuit,*" Dante said.

"What?"

"Night is feminine in French. *De la nuit.*"

I rolled my eyes. "Looks like someone chose Rosetta Stone over the crotch fiddle."

Dante's face flushed, and his fangs retracted suddenly. I could almost see the memory of his blood mishap from the night before playing out behind his eyes. I wondered if the princess ever felt this wretched after pushing my buttons. Maybe that was why she rushed off so soon after each time.

"I should go," I said, standing.

"Jenna." Dante stepped in front of me. His touch was feather-light on my shoulder, but my skin warmed as his fingers trailed down the back of my arm. The manic look in his eyes faded into a softer expression. "It is more than just Ursula. I...I could not bear it if—"

A sharp knock cut him off, and then Belinda's muffled voice echoed through the double doors. "Your Grace?" she called excitedly.

Dante withdrew his hand and ground his teeth. "Enter!" He bit off the word so harshly that I jumped.

A door cracked open, and Belinda poked her head inside. "Forgive me for intruding, but Captain Nicks just called. One of his units picked up the missing girls from Darkly Hall here in St. Louis." Her smile hinted that they were in better condition than Jodie Watts. "They're on their way now."

Dante's shoulders sagged with relief. He raked a hand through his hair and licked his lips. "Once they arrive, bring them to me straight away."

"Yes, Your Grace." Belinda bowed her head before exiting and closing the door behind her.

I waited for Dante to finish what he'd been saying before the interruption. But instead, he turned to stare out the darkened wall of windows behind the fireplace and hugged himself.

"That's great news," I said, trying to mean it. "Looks like that just leaves Ingrid unaccounted for."

Dante nodded slowly. His mind had wandered off somewhere I couldn't follow, and I suddenly felt like I was invading his privacy. I didn't want to be here when his new blood bride and her donors-in-waiting arrived. But before I managed to work up the nerve to leave, Dante turned around again, facing me.

"I sincerely wanted this for you," he said, following the comment with a disappointed sigh.

"Wanted *what* for me?" My stomach did a somersault as I swallowed.

"Your reinstatement with Blood Vice." He gave me an odd look that made me wonder if he knew the direction my mind had initially gone. "But even if Ursula had the courage for it, I fear I do not."

"What's that supposed to mean?"

Dante's chestnut eyes were tender, even as they filled with

irony. "What do you think it means, Ms. Skye?"

My breath picked up speed, as did my pulse. Maybe all our flirty banter wasn't as frivolous as I'd imagined. Though, I wasn't sure how to feel about that or where we went with it from here. I opened my mouth, preparing to free all the delicate questions I'd been hoarding.

But then another knock came at the door before it opened without an invitation, halting my inquiry.

"Audrey." Dante brushed past me, and I turned to watch him cross the room and greet the newcomer with a warm hug.

She was…*gorgeous*. No other word would do. Her face was clean, not a speck of makeup, and she wore a pastel green dress that looked as if it had been stolen off the back of a Southern belle. Strawberry curls dusted her pale shoulders just inside the wide, lace collar of her dress.

"Your Grace," she sighed breathlessly and curtseyed as Dante released her.

"Are you all right? Should I call for the harem nurse?" He touched her cheek, and she blushed, turning her face away coyly. I instantly hated her.

"I am fine—we all are," she said, nodding over her shoulder at a pair of young ladies waiting in the hallway. "Whatever our captors' intentions were, they were unable to fulfill them before Polly escaped and called for help. Your brave men rescued us mere moments later. Bless them."

Dante nodded. "I will see to it that they each receive personal recognition and a handsome Midwinter bonus."

Audrey yawned against the back of her dainty hand. "A thousand apologies, Your Grace. It's been a terribly long night."

He smiled softly and cupped her shoulders. "Of course, my dear."

My fangs dug into my bottom lip. I had to get out of there.

Belinda and Yoshiko appeared out in the hall with the two other girls. More curtseys and bows were exchanged, and I decided that I wouldn't be playing Miss Manners with anyone tonight.

I was a duchess of House Lilith, however useless or temporary the title was, and if Ursula's etiquette lessons had taught me anything, it was that the only people I was absolutely required to stoop to were the queen, the prince, and the princess. Everyone else could suck an egg. I was in no mood. Not after watching Dante fawn over his new blood bride.

"My harem manager will show your donors-in-waiting to their quarters upstairs," the duke said, eliciting another bow from Yoshiko. "And Belinda, my assistant, will show you to your room in the south wing."

So I was acquiring a fancy new neighbor. *Great.*

"We can talk more tonight, after sunset," Dante said to Audrey, leading her out into the hallway to hand off to Belinda.

He hadn't bothered to introduce me, and Audrey hadn't so much as looked in my direction. I felt like a fly on the wall. *More like in the ointment*, I decided when the virgin blood doll shot me a fleeting glance. She was probably wondering if I was the duke's midnight snack.

When Dante closed the door behind the dispersing crowd in the hallway, I cleared my throat, reminding him that I was still there.

"I really should go and get cleaned up," I said, cutting across the room to where he stood. "Ursula will come looking for me soon."

"Yes," he agreed. "She would skin me alive if she knew the danger you were in tonight."

"A thousand apologies, *Your Grace*," I said, mimicking Audrey's sticky-sweet, Southern accent.

He blinked at me, lips parting with surprise. "You're jealous."

"Am I?" I sidestepped around him, but he caught my arm before I reached the doors.

"I am following the queen's orders," Dante said softly. "This new bond has no bearing on the one I share with you."

"And what bond is it that you think we share?" I huffed

and pulled my arm out of his grasp. When he hesitated to answer, I went for the exit again. "You know what? Forget I asked."

"Jenna—"

I circled around the back hallway and cut down the south wing, relieved to see that all the bedroom doors were closed. I'd figure out which one I needed to avoid tomorrow. For now, a cold shower was in order.

Dante's new arm candy might have had a long night, but mine wasn't even close to being over. Though I doubted the second half would be any more pleasant than the first.

Chapter Nine

I didn't see much of Dante over the next few days. It was my own fault. I stayed holed up in my room, letting the harem staff deliver my blood, and I even skipped out on the gym sessions with Murphy. Other than watching Laura's soap with Mandy, I mostly read etiquette and poetry books. The only time I ventured out was for the sessions with Ursula in the library.

The princess didn't even complain about my lack of focus. She was distracted herself, with the upcoming ball and the household wardrobe Dante had put entirely in her hands. Though, as the week dragged on, she shifted her attention back to my etiquette lessons.

We met earlier than usual Thursday night, since the tailor would be arriving soon after, and Ursula wanted to be present for each fitting. She, Dante, Audrey, and I would be wearing more elaborate getups, but Mandy, Murphy, Audrey's dowry donors, and a handful of other guards and donors would also be outfitted in matching attire.

We were to make a strong, elegant showing to prevent the vultures of night society from targeting us as prey. Ursula's paranoia had needed a more constructive outlet. Dante had been wise to assign the ball attire to her. Basket case or not, the princess knew fashion—and she wasn't so far gone that she'd consider accessorizing us with tinfoil hats.

I wanted to be excited about the ball. But any time I thought about it, all I could picture was Dante and Audrey together. Dancing in the queen's ballroom. Greeting the other fancy vamps. I imagined that Audrey knew a dozen different waltzes, and she'd probably been studying the who's who of vamp society since she was twelve.

"Have you heard a single thing I've said?" The tone of Ursula's voice crossed into dangerous territory, and I sat upright at the library table.

"I'm sorry," I said. "I must have zoned out. What was the question?"

Ursula snorted and leaned against a bookcase near the window. Laughter and splashing filtered in through the glass, and she turned to steal a glance at the pool below. It was heated, so Dante hadn't winterized it yet.

"She's a pretty little thing, isn't she?" Ursula said. "Dante says she's an exceptional pianist, too. He's having a baby grand delivered for her. Darkly Hall certainly covers all their bases."

"Do you play anything?" I asked, eager to steer the conversation away from Audrey.

Ursula shot me an impish grin before turning back to the window. "My human father sang in Mozart's chorus. After the great concertmaster's passing in Vienna, I was shipped to the States to sing for Raynor Taylor."

"You must have been good," I said, still digesting the fact that she'd been alive during Mozart's time. "How did you end up at a blood finishing school?"

"Chasing a girl." A hiccup of a laugh escaped her. "How else? A few years later, I sang for Morgan. The rest is history." She sat on the bench in front of the window and sighed. "You don't seem to have much interest in music. I would have requested more drawing supplies on your behalf, but you haven't done much of that lately either."

I shrugged, unable to offer a valid excuse. "Does the duke sing or play an instrument?"

"Dante's always been fond of his cameras—and the sun. His sire, Alexander, wasn't musically inclined either. Lili found him in the theater. Talent—or at least passion—is important when you have forever ahead of you."

"I've never heard you sing before," I said, propping my chin in one hand.

"And you never will." The light in Ursula's eyes dimmed. "The last song I sang was for Morgan. My music died with her."

I didn't know what to say to that. I looked down at the open etiquette book I'd smuggled back into the library before our lesson. Maybe I didn't know how to sing or play piano, but at least I wouldn't be falling on my face at the ball. And perhaps I could stand to brush up on what artistic talent I had, too.

"Could I...draw you sometime?" I asked Ursula. She looked perplexed by the question, one perfectly groomed eyebrow arching suggestively.

"Like one of your French girls?"

"I was thinking clothed. Maybe a fancy gown," I said in a flat tone. Ursula smirked at me and glanced out the window again as more noise bubbled up from the pool.

"Perhaps tomorrow. The fittings will take some time, and I'd like to go for a swim before Dante seals everything up for the season."

I stood and joined her, spying on the party below. Audrey and one of her dowry donors tossed a beach ball back and forth in the water with a pair of donors I recognized from the harem. The duke's pending scion wore a vintage bathing suit with polka dots. Her hair was pulled back and styled into Dutch braids that ended in a bun at the base of her neck. She was catalog perfect.

Her other donor-in-waiting watched from a lounge chair, a closed book in her lap. Worry crinkled her features, but anytime Audrey looked up at her from the pool, she smiled and waved.

"Poor thing," Ursula commented.

"Poor thing?" I stared at the princess. "What does she

have to be so anxious about? Isn't this what they signed up for? Isn't this what they *trained* for?"

Ursula shrugged. "Trained or not, she's waiting for her friend to die so she can be her first meal. Wouldn't you be anxious?"

I pressed my lips together and looked out the window again as guilt knotted my stomach. Maybe I could find it in myself to be nice to the new humans in the house. After all, they were here for Audrey to snack on, not Dante.

"I'm going to send one of the guards out to fetch some quality drawing paper and charcoals before tomorrow night," Ursula said. "Hopefully, Dante will have a suitable frame in that studio of his."

"Frame?" I shook my head. "I was just going to break in one of the new sketchpads."

She lifted her chin. "My scion's first portrait of me will be properly preserved for centuries to come. I'll not have it any other way—"

"Okay, okay," I said before the pitch of her voice rose any higher.

She headed for the library door, but then paused and turned back to me. "That will be all for your lessons tonight. I'll see you in Dante's office when the tailor arrives."

I blinked at her, surprised that she'd said anything at all. Let alone something nice. "Uh, yup. I mean, *yes*, Your

Highness." The words felt odd in my mouth, saying them without sarcasm or in fear for my life.

Ursula seemed just as surprised as I was. She nodded slowly and then slipped out of the library, leaving me standing there in a confused daze.

I scooped up the most recent etiquette book I'd been secretly studying in my room and made a poetry sandwich out of it again. The familiar routine was habit now, though it wasn't necessary. I'd yet to bump into anyone who cared about my selection of books on the way back to my room. The guards who knew and liked me never offered more than a passing smile or nod—except for Murphy.

Thinking of him made me feel like a jerk. We hadn't spoken since we returned from Bathory House. I assumed he was mad at me for whatever trouble I'd gotten him into with the duke. But angry or not, I considered him my friend. I should have checked in on him by now.

I glanced down at my watch as I stepped out of the library and headed for the north-wing stairwell. Murphy would be finishing up in the gym about now. I had enough time to swing by there before stashing my books and getting changed for the fitting.

Ursula had given me a slip and petticoat to wear for the tailoring. She'd also picked out a pair of tights and heeled boots that laced up to just above my ankles. Those were required for the fitting, as well, since she was so particular about the exact length off the floor a dress should be.

I also wanted to fix my hair and makeup before crossing paths with Dante again.

I had this nervous surge of panic whenever I thought of our last conversation. I didn't know what to make of our...*bond.* I was impatient with Dante one second, and hesitant the next. He seemed to have the same problem, and I was just as aggravated with him as I was with myself over it. Were we playing hard-to-get or taking things slow? Were we doing *anything* at all? *Should* we be doing anything at all?

And like clockwork, just as soon as those thoughts lit up my mind, so did Roman's face. A part of me desperately hoped I'd find him at the queen's ball. A more selfish part of me hoped Vanessa would keep him at the bat cave with her forever. Then I wouldn't have to make up excuses for the feelings I had for the man who had simultaneously killed him and ended our affair.

The decision had also saved me from an extra-long coffin nap. So, there was *that*.

I pushed the guilt aside to make room for more as I reached the gym. As I stepped inside the room, I heard Murphy's familiar, husky voice.

"Is that the best you got?" he howled at another guy in the ring with him. They bounced on their toes, dodging and ducking punches. Then Murphy's eyes darted across the room to where I stood by the door, and he froze. His opponent took the opportunity to clock him across the jaw.

I winced and sucked in a hissing breath. "Ouch."

The other guy spun around and gaped at me. He spat his mouthguard into his open hand and backed into a corner as Murphy dragged himself to his feet.

"Oh, man! I thought you were trying to pull a fast one on me. I-I'm so sorry, Murph," he stammered.

"It's all good," Murphy said, rubbing his face. "It's about time for me to call it quits anyway."

"Same time tomorrow?"

"Sure," Murphy answered, shooting me a sideways glance.

Of course he'd replaced me as his sparring partner. He was a guard. This wasn't a hobby for him. He was required to stay sharp as a member of the duke's security detail. I swallowed and tried to smile at him.

"What can I do you for, Skye?" Murphy asked as the other guard grabbed up his gym bag and climbed down off the raised platform. The man wiped the sweat from his face and nodded politely at me as he walked past on his way out the door.

I shrugged. "I just wanted to apologize for bailing on you these past few days—and for any trouble you may have gotten into over the Bathory House incident."

Murphy snorted and grabbed his towel off the corner post before sitting on the edge of the platform. He folded his arms over one of the coated ropes that lined the ring. "I might be imagining things here, but I think the boss has a soft spot for you. He wasn't even this uptight after the trash truck park battle."

I whispered out a nervous laugh and looked down at the books tucked under my arm, my other hand covering the titles down their spines. "It's because I'm Ursula's scion now."

"Is that right?" Murphy teased. "I'd completely forgotten, Your Grace." He twirled a hand in the air and bowed his head. "Your princess organized a little class for the guards and donors attending the ball. We're to express our loyalties and admiration liberally and deliberately," he said with a dry grin.

"Good grief." I rolled my eyes. "She's taking this etiquette business a little far, don't you think?"

He cocked his head from side to side and then touched his jaw again, tenderly. "If this bruises before I have to play dress-up with her tonight, she'll probably order me to stop boxing until after the big party."

"Maybe she'll just recommend a little makeup," I offered, earning a horrified look from him.

"Don't go giving her any ideas now," he said, running his towel over his short hair and flicking sweat in my direction. "I thought we were friends, Skye."

"Are we?" I asked, only half-joking. "Can I still come over to play? Will your new friend mind?"

"Please." He made a face at me. "You know what time I'm here. You're always welcome."

I smiled. "If I'm able to show my face around here after this fitting, you can count on seeing me tomorrow."

"Ditto," Murphy said, his eyebrows hitching with concern.

By the time I had changed and made it to Dante's office—temporarily converted to accommodate the tailor— Ursula's moment of civility had passed. She gave my slip and petticoat an affronted once-over.

"I realize it's more modest than you're accustomed to, but it's still underwear, dear. You could have at least put a maxi dress over it."

"Sorry," I mumbled, suddenly grateful that Dante wasn't present. His little blood bride probably knew better than to waltz around the manor half-dressed.

Ursula gave my attempt at makeup an even more unsavory scowl. "We'll have the harem manager take care of...*that* on the night of the ball," she said, waving a finger at my face.

"I've never seen Yoshiko wear makeup," I said, wondering if Ursula knew what she was talking about. I couldn't remember ever seeing her interact with the donors outside of ordering them to fetch her blood, but I kept that note to myself.

"She doesn't anymore, but she's had the proper training," Ursula said before edging out of the tailor's way.

"I am Ethan, Your Grace," the man said, bowing his head briefly before motioning for me to lift my arms so he could wrap a corset around my midsection. After squeezing my waist into an unnaturally small circumference, he added a second petticoat over the first. Then, finally, he helped me into the gown.

After the falling-out with House Novak, Ursula hadn't even attempted to request their services. But, she assured me more than once, House Vionnet was older and more renowned. She'd flown in one of their best, and several assistants, from France and put them up in a presidential suite at the Nightfall Opera House.

Dante had several empty guest rooms in the south wing, but crafting numerous elaborate garments required more workspace. Ethan Vionnet had brought his own machines and dress forms, a zillion rolls of fabric, and baskets full of lace and beads for Ursula to choose from. He was determined to give the princess exactly what she wanted. And now that she'd been given access to the family fortune again, she was willing to pay out the nose for it.

"Too much lace," Ursula snapped as Ethan held a section up across my chest where the raw hem of the dress collar stopped. "But I like the fringed edge. Maybe if you ruffle it and stitch it under the collar, almost like a modesty panel— minus the modesty because I'd like to see some cleavage— not too much, though. Keep it tasteful."

Ethan's hands shook as he attempted to follow her instructions just as fast as she spat them out. He accidentally poked me with a pin as he folded the collar of my dress down an inch lower, and I inhaled sharply through my nose. *Sorry,* he mouthed, giving me a pained smile.

Ursula paused to dig through one of the baskets he'd brought. She fished out a roll of black lace and a chiffon rosette. "We want to toe the line between Queen Victoria and Moulin Rouge," she said as she turned around and held the sheer rose up to my shoulder and then to my hair. "Some feathers might be nice. What do you think, my scion?"

I glanced at the folding panel of mirrors propped against Dante's desk and admired the sea of green and black the princess had chosen for the color palette. "Ten points to Slytherin."

Ursula blinked stiffly. "Should I assume that's a

compliment?"

"Assume away." When she continued to stare at me, I added, "It's perfection."

"Ah, I like that answer much better," she said, then glanced at the clock on the far wall. "Audrey will be here shortly. Once Ethan's finished pinning your gown, you may disrobe and resume your evening. I'm going to check in with Dante to see if he has any input to offer on his new blood doll's attire."

"Yes, Your Highness." I nodded my head slightly, careful not to move too much as Ethan finished adjusting my collar. He paused long enough to cock his head at Ursula, as well.

"Highness," he said around the pins tucked in one corner of his mouth.

Ursula left through one of the double doors that led into the front foyer, and I watched Ethan's shoulders drop from under his ears.

"You're doing great," I said, his visible anxiety dragging the compliment out of me. "Really, this is the nicest dress I've ever worn."

Ethan plucked the remaining pins from his mouth and smiled. "*Merci*. This is my first ensemble in America. I want it to be *magnifique*."

He helped me out of the dress, and I left the office, quickly heading back to my room in hopes of avoiding

Audrey. Laura's soap would be on soon, and I had a book about proper eye contact and curtseys to finish. *Barf.*

I was going to have to get over my problem with Dante's pending scion soon…or find better reading material. Maybe take up one of those damn hobbies the duke kept suggesting.

Chapter Ten

At the Duke of House Lilith's manor, socializing took place either in the gym or the harem lounge. The guards mostly stuck to the gym, and the donors to the lounge, but there was a handful who cross-pollinated. Murphy and I both did, but Mandy was probably the most integrated between the two crowds.

She and Yoshiko had bonded over their love of video games, and come Friday night, I'd let Mandy talk me into inviting her to watch Laura's soap in my bedroom with us after a round of sparring with Murphy. Yoshiko returned the favor by inviting us upstairs for smoothies—and blood for me.

"Pew, pew! Die!" Mandy screamed at the big screen as she mashed buttons on one of the video game controllers. Her high ponytail flopped on top of her head as she squirmed on the sofa, using her whole body to play.

"You first! Ha!" Yoshiko replied from the opposite end of the couch. I was squeezed between them, getting bounced and bumped all over the place.

"Noooo!" Mandy wailed, her character spewing teeth and blood as Yoshiko's avatar delivered a throat punch followed by a kicking cartwheel of an uppercut.

I watched wide-eyed as I slurped my blood cocktail

through a stainless-steel straw. Yoshiko had prepared my beverage to match hers and Mandy's—in a glass with a little umbrella—for a change of scenery, she'd said. Without tapping a vein, this was the most variety I'd had in quite some time. I appreciated the effort.

"Welp," Yoshiko said, hopping up from the sofa with a victorious grin. "Who's ready for seconds?"

"As long as you're talking smoothies and not ass-kickings," Mandy grumbled.

"And blood," I added, shaking my empty glass.

Yoshiko opened her arms in a theatrical gesture toward the kitchen at the other end of the lounge. "This way, mighty warriors!"

Mandy and I followed her across the room, each taking a barstool as she circled the long counter. The lounge was mostly deserted at this hour—the quote, unquote *breakfast* rush for the vamps in the house. Most of the donors were either feeding guards or delivering blood pots downstairs.

The fresh bite on Yoshiko's neck—and the extra wide grin on her face—told me that she'd fed Murphy recently. She touched the spot fondly before fetching a teapot in a pumpkin-colored cozy from the stove along the back counter.

"So, what do you think of the new girls?" I asked, finally feeling brave enough to drop the question. It didn't sound half as casual out loud as it had in my head.

Yoshiko's eyes darted up to me before her attention returned to fixing my drink. "They're nice."

"That's...vague," Mandy said, digging a rogue strawberry out of her glass with her straw.

Yoshiko took a deep breath as she handed me the fresh blood. Then she moved down to the sink where she'd left the blender pitcher to dry earlier. "Truthfully, I haven't spent much time with them yet. They prefer to keep their mistress company in her room downstairs. Ronan and Tara said they had fun with them in the pool, though."

"Hmm." I sipped at my glass of blood to hide my frown.

"Their names are Polly and Kate," Yoshiko added, sensing my disappointment. "I'm sure you've already met Audrey. They grew up together in West Texas, in a traditional donor community, and then studied together at Darkly Hall for eight years. It's one of the top-rated schools in the country."

I refrained from rolling my eyes. "Any word if Blood Vice found their *captors*, as the blood bride-to-be referred to them?"

Yoshiko shook her head. "Only Polly got a look, but it was dark, and she was more interested in the license plate number and locating a phone to call for help."

"Fast-thinker," Mandy said, impressed.

"Darkly trains them for crisis situations," Yoshiko added. "I'm surprised the duke didn't start there, but I suppose he was trying to strengthen his more local business connections."

"So, did you study at a blood finishing school?" I asked, trying to balance the gossip with acceptable conversation—per Ursula's lesson on how to be a busybody the *proper* way.

Yoshiko blushed and turned her back to us, placing the pitcher back on the blender base. "I did, a long time ago."

"Which one?" I couldn't picture Yoshiko in a place like Bathory House, with their strange, cultish restrictions and cookie-cutter look. Plus, Ursula had said that Yoshiko has been trained in how to apply makeup. Bathory House didn't do makeup. The Southern belle scene at Darkly Hall didn't seem to fit quite right either.

"Does it matter?" Yoshiko asked.

"I didn't get to attend," I said. "Humor me."

She dug a bag of frozen berries and the coconut milk out of the refrigerator and put some of each into the blender. Next, she grabbed a banana from a hanging basket under the cabinets. The good cheer had abandoned her expression, and she avoided eye contact as she finished adding ingredients to the blender.

"Yeah, Yosh," Mandy said, her curiosity just as piqued as mine. "Tell us. I want to hear all about your glamorous time at charm school."

Mandy's introduction to supernatural society hadn't been any more informative or kind than mine. What didn't kill you made you stronger—and confused as hell. We both wanted to know what it was like to be given a choice and an instruction manual for this alarming new existence.

"The Blood Okiya in L.A.," Yoshiko finally answered. Then she pressed down the lid on the pitcher and hit the power button. As the air buzzed with white noise, Mandy and I exchanged curious glances.

When Yoshiko stopped the blender, I asked, "Isn't that the one exclusively for the Blood House Geishas?"

"It is." Yoshiko nodded absently. "I shed a lot of blood, sweat, and tears training to be one of them."

"But then how—?"

"I was dismissed." She put the pitcher of smoothie down so hard that it splashed over the edge of the container. Purple goop dripped from the counter and onto the floor, but Yoshiko grabbed a dishrag from the sink and set to work cleaning the mess. "I was terrible at playing the shamisen, terrible at dancing, and I botched my first performance as a *maiko*—in front of the duke. When the *okā-san* fired me on the spot, knowing my family would never take me back, Dante hired me."

"Oh…" I tried to picture Yoshiko as one of the painted geishas I'd seen at the fancy vamp party Roman had taken me to last year before I went through training to be a Blood Vice agent. He'd told me that they ate special diets to flavor their blood, but other than that, they were traditionally trained geishas.

Ursula's coverage of the fat bats in the vamp world hadn't revealed much more. The geishas in California were all Japanese Americans from the same community in Torrance. They operated several teahouses in L.A. but also flew all over the world to entertain at parties hosted by rich and famous bloodsuckers. The original Blood Okiya was still in Kyoto, but they had branched out to several other countries in addition to the States.

"You know," Mandy said, leaning over the counter to reach the smoothie pitcher, "that duke is starting to grow on me. He's an all right guy."

Yoshiko nodded and held her glass out, letting Mandy refill it. "He really is."

"I'll third that," I said, toasting their smoothies with my blood.

I meant it, too.

As much as I could hate the duke for Roman's sake, I adored Dante for so much more.

I didn't know how it had taken me so long to recognize it for what it was, but I suddenly realized that Dante was a bleeding heart. Yoshiko, Ursula, me... He collected lost causes and gave us a second chance.

And I was willing to bet that we weren't the only ones at

the manor who owed him a debt we could never repay.

Ursula skipped our nightly lesson in favor of beginning her portrait. I should have known that stoking the flames of her vanity would be the easiest way to ditch class. Although, her company was only mildly less infuriating.

"Over there," she directed Murphy, pointing for him to leave the kerosene lamp he carried on top of the low bookcase that divided the library in half. "Now, be gone."

"Thank you," I said as Murphy walked past me. The crease between his brows softened, and he dipped his head in a subtle nod before making his exit.

According to the princess, using artificial lighting was unacceptable for crafting a masterpiece. Two more oil lamps rested at the far end of the long table where she usually conducted our lessons. They provided just enough light for me to see what I was doing with the supplies she'd had delivered.

A huge sheet of thick, textured paper had been clipped to an easel. Several hand towels and an array of pencils, brushes, charcoals, smudge sticks, and pastels lay along the edge of the table. There were also several jars of water and mineral spirits, all arranged on a plastic sheet. I hardly knew where to begin.

"Well?" Ursula said. She stood in front of the window, the glow of the lanterns reflecting off the glass behind her. "Do you have everything you need?"

I nodded. "And then some."

The gown she'd chosen was a blue so pale it was almost gray. The neckline cut a sharp line just beneath her collarbones, and the shimmery fabric hugged her until it reached the bends of her elbows and knees, where it ended in loose, lace ruffles.

"Where do you want me?" she asked, glancing at her reflection in the window behind her.

"Wherever. Just make sure it's a comfortable position that you're able to stay in for a while."

Ursula sniffed and sat down, propping her arms on the back of the bench. She folded her legs and tilted up her chin, the epitome of regal confidence. "You may begin."

"Yes, Your Highness," I said, struggling to keep the sarcasm out of my tone. If she hadn't caught my *Harry Potter* joke, I doubted she'd appreciate an *Alice in Wonderland*-type inflection.

Among the supplies, I noticed a set of oil pastels. I'd stuck to charcoal in my sketchbook. It had been a long time since I worked with anything else, but I was tempted. While I considered my options, I picked up a gray colored pencil and did a light sketch first, figuring out the scale and proportions.

Despite her high-maintenance personality, Ursula was a model art subject. Maybe it had something to do with being an old vamp, a throwback to a long-gone era of elegance and discipline. She sat statue-still, holding the angle of her chin firmly in place and maintaining intense eye contact with me. She clearly wanted this done right. As soon as I started in with the oil pastels, I realized that she was correct about the lighting, too.

The warmth of the firelight gave new depths to her skin and traced bold highlights in her hair and eyes. Her pale dress held a full spectrum of shadows, and the darkened window created a striking contrast. I tried not to rush as I captured it all, taking extra care with the finer details.

It wasn't quite like riding a bicycle, but slowly, I began to remember the various tricks and techniques I'd learned in high school. An hour turned into two, but I kept going, my fingers stained to the knuckles from blending, and sweat dotting my brow from the workout such a large piece required.

When I was satisfied with the portrait, I nodded to Ursula. "You can blink now."

"Finally." She sighed and let her arms fall to the cushioned bench. Then she stood and crossed the library, stopping beside me to examine the finished product. After a long moment of silent scrutiny, she nodded once. "That will do. Frame and deliver it to my room before sunrise."

I gave her a tight-lipped smile, annoyed by her rudeness but no longer surprised. "Yes, Your Highness."

On her way out of the library, she once again paused, turning back to me as if an afterthought. "Well done, my scion."

They hadn't taught us how to professionally frame drawings and paintings in my high school art class. If the teacher deemed something good enough for the annual art show, she just taped it to some pre-cut mat board. But, I'd harassed Dante about Blood Vice and Ursula enough times in his studio that I had a general idea of how it should work for something more appropriate for the princess's bedroom wall.

I removed the portrait from the easel and held it by the top corners as I carried it downstairs. Two guards stood sentry in the foyer on either side of the double doors to the duke's office, a sure sign that he was working. Neither of them stopped me as I ducked down the back hallway. The doorknob to the studio was difficult to work with my elbow, but I eventually managed to fumble it open and laid the portrait down on the worktable before turning on the overhead light.

The room was more intimidating than I remembered with its massive printing machines and strange collection of tools. I went to the back wall first, where dozens of frames hung from long pegs. Most of them were simple and solid black—perfect for the sunrise and sunset photographs Dante liked to take. But some were more intricate and painted in a variety of metallic hues. I chose a deep copper-colored frame with ivy etchings for Ursula's portrait.

On a shelf under the work table, I found a piece of museum glass that fit the frame and then used it as a template to cut a matching piece of backer board. I was deep in thought, trying to figure out what came next when someone knocked on the open door. I nearly jumped out of my skin.

"Didn't mean to frighten you," Audrey giggled. She stood in the doorway, wearing a white tulle skirt and a navy cashmere sweater. It was an improvement over the plantation gown, but it didn't make me like her any better. She held up a hand in peaceful surrender, and I noticed two tiny puncture marks on her wrist. That didn't make me like her any more.

"I wasn't *frightened*," I snapped. "I was startled. Completely different."

"Then I apologize for *startling* you," she said, completely unfazed by my spitefulness. "We haven't been properly introduced. I'm Audrey Moore, the duke's future scion."

"I know," I replied, sounding even more juvenile than I

had before. "What do you want?"

"Oh, I just found my friend's bracelet in the hallway," she said, holding up her other hand. "I was on my way to return it to her when I saw the studio light on…" Her voice trailed off as I turned my back on her and ducked down to grab a piece of mat board from the shelf under the table.

"Well, now you know it's me. Mystery solved." I found a yardstick and measured off where I wanted the matting to lay over the portrait. When I turned around, Audrey was still lingering in the doorway, delicate hands folded over her heart. I glanced down at my own, at the pastels caked under my nails and in the creases of my knuckles.

"Is there anything I can do to help?" Audrey asked.

"No."

"*Oh*. Okay…"

"Did you need something else?" I blinked at her, wondering if she was having a territorial issue about Dante's favorite room in the manor.

Audrey smiled weakly. "We're going to be family soon, and we'll be living together for some time I've been told."

I grimaced at the reminder. "I'm aware."

"Have I done something to displease you?" she asked, matching my expression with a sour one of her own. "Please, tell me if I have. I will gladly make whatever amends are required."

"Wow. I didn't realize Darkly Hall specialized in people-pleasers," I scoffed and turned back to the table, trying to remember what I'd been looking for. *A utility knife.* That was it. I found one in a wire basket hanging from the pegboard behind the table.

"Darkly Hall teaches us to respect and cherish family," Audrey said defensively. "Especially our immortal family."

"Then why don't you show a little respect and leave me alone." I waved a hand down at the unassembled frame. "Can't you see I'm busy?"

Her doe eyes watered, but she offered a parting curtsey. "Yes, Your Grace," she said and then turned and left.

I finished framing Ursula's portrait in silence, stewing over what an asshat the girl had turned me into—over what an asshat *I* had turned myself into. She'd flustered me with her bubbly, eager-beaver personality, but that wasn't a good enough reason to bite her head off.

I wondered what a good enough reason would be. The guilty knot in my gut tightened, but I ignored it as I left the studio and headed for Ursula's room, the finished portrait in hand. My pride had been dampened by Audrey's visit, but I still admired the piece. It sparked something in me that I hadn't felt for some time.

I decided that I'd have to do this again soon. Maybe for Mandy or Murphy. Perhaps even the duke.

Chapter Eleven

It had been almost a week since I'd last seen Dante. Which I'd come to find...*rare* since Imbolc. He'd go on overnight trips, be gone for two or three days at a time, but he'd always come to find me before he left and again after he returned. And our paths seemed to cross at least every other day whenever he was home. Sometimes, I'd drop in on him. Sometimes, he'd drop in on me.

I'd been waiting for him to make the first move, my pride still bruised from our last conversation. But he seemed to be doing the same thing. Or else he'd entirely forgotten about me, distracted by his perfect new pet.

I wondered how the investigations were going for the potential scions who hadn't made it this far. I'd pestered Murphy a few times, but he didn't seem to know anything— nothing he was willing or able to share with me anyway. As far as I knew, Ingrid was still missing. It wasn't a good sign.

But I also wondered what would happen if she turned up alive. Would Dante send Audrey back to Austin? Or Ingrid back to Belleville? Would he keep them both? Would I lose my mind with double the envy?

The weekend passed by in an uneventful blur without even Laura's show to look forward to. Mandy was home, but she'd picked up a few extra guard shifts while one of the duke's wolves was on paternity leave. And then, Monday night, Murphy caught up with me before our usual sparring time to cancel.

The ball was scheduled for next Wednesday, and the attending security detail was meeting up to go over protocol and to re-test their firearm accuracy in the underground range that split off from the basement and ran the length of the north wing under the gym and garage.

Something that I somehow hadn't heard about until now.

I knew the duke wouldn't be attending this meeting. He trusted Murphy to captain his royal guard. And since I was going to be at the ball anyway, and I knew my way around a pistol or two, there was no reason why I shouldn't have been invited to this gathering and allowed to sharpen up in their fancy range.

That—and a little begging—was how I ended up crammed in a tiny office full of beefy vampires and werewolves in the basement of the manor. Murphy stood in front of a whiteboard at the back of the room. At the last minute, Mandy joined us, nudging in between another guard and me. I didn't have time to question her before Murphy began his lecture.

"Listen up, men—and ladies. The security system is scheduled for an update later this evening. That means overlapping perimeter shifts. If you have questions, save them for after the meeting so no one is late reporting for duty. If you don't have time to re-test on the range tonight, I expect you to make time tomorrow night. Anyone who doesn't will be dismissed from this assignment."

A few of the guards shuffled uneasily, occasionally glancing down at their watches, but they didn't say anything. I'd already witnessed what a tight ship the duke ran. I didn't imagine he made exceptions for meetings or office birthday parties.

"We have five major priorities next Wednesday," Murphy continued, ticking them off on his fingers as he listed them. "The duke, the princess, the duchess, the future baroness, and the harem. We're allowed a night guard and a daylight attendant for each of the royals. Four vamps and four wolves. The queen's estate will be heavily fortified, so our biggest concern will be the transport to and from Denver." He paused to stare Mandy and me down. "This should go without saying, but just in case there's any doubt, this is confidential information. The boss's house has many enemies. Let's not make our jobs harder than they have to be."

"Here, here!" a guard in the back shouted. Several others chuckled under their breaths.

Murphy cleared his throat and turned to the dry erase board, drawing two large rectangles and two smaller ones. Inside the first rectangle, he wrote several names in what I assumed was another language, considering how hard it was to read.

"Lane will take the first SUV with two wolves and three of the donors we're bringing from the harem for the royal fam," he said as the dry erase marker squeaked across the board. "Guards will be sticking to the queen's blood stock for the party to reduce the size of the harem we're traveling with. It's safer, and since we'll be taking the private jet, we're limited on available seats."

Private jet? First, there's a shooting range in the basement, and now a private jet? I definitely wasn't asking the right questions. I side-eyed Mandy, curious to see if she'd known about either.

In the second large rectangle, Murphy wrote more names. "SUV number two. A vamp, a wolf, three donors. Donnie will drive the duke and the future baroness. That leaves the princess, the duchess, and Starsgard with me. There will be just enough seats for the guards who'll be driving the fleet back to the manor," he finished, scribbling our names in the smaller boxes in illegible chicken scratch.

I should have expected that the duke would want his little protégé in the same car as him, but it didn't ease my disappointment—and it effectively spoiled the distraction I had hoped this meeting might offer.

Murphy cleared his throat, dragging my attention back to the whiteboard. "Drivers will meet with me Friday evening for a test run to the airport. House McCoy is providing us an identical rental fleet for our stay in Denver, so we'll load up the same way once we land."

I wasn't sure if this was how all major outings were planned, or if this was an extra precaution being taken since the trash truck park battle, but every guard in the room was paying attention. These were professionals, and even if their days were vastly ho-hum, they were paid well to always be aware of potential threats. Mindful of their surroundings. To be on time, even if they knew they'd likely spend the next twelve hours walking through the dark with only the crickets for company.

Mandy was right there with them, fully absorbing the information and not catching a single glance I shot her—unless she was ignoring me on purpose, knowing I had some serious questions about what else she'd been hiding since being initiated into the guard squad.

Why on earth wouldn't she have told me about the shooting range under the manor? Was she sworn to secrecy? Had the guards taught her their secret handshake and told her that I wasn't allowed in the club? Or was my duchess tempus status really such a big deal now that even Mandy saw me as some fragile, helpless thing?

Murphy went on to cover the emergency procedures in the event of a plane crash, and then rattled off an everyone-is-dangerous-at-this-party speech that I imagined he'd given plenty of times before. After that, we finally filed out of his office and headed to the range. Half of the men split off and went upstairs to begin their shifts, leaving Murphy, Mandy, me, and two wolves who likely had day shift.

We passed a couple of halls lined with doors on either side that I assumed were the guards' living quarters, and then several closed doors all labeled: *storeroom*. The concrete walls were thicker at this end of the basement, narrowing the hallway that curled around a bend and led to a solid steel door with a small viewing window.

Inside, eight shooting booths were angled down a cavernous tunnel. Rails lined the ceiling, curling just ahead of each cubical where stacks of silhouette targets hung, ready to go. Which was good, since *I* was ready to go. It had been too long since I'd squeezed a trigger, and I needed some catharsis.

Now that I had my guns and gear back, I'd made a few adjustments to my old, double shoulder holster so it would accommodate the pair of Reaper TDs that Dante had given me before Ursula's trial. I'd worn my blazer to cover the arsenal, just in case the princess's aversion to exposed undergarments extended to open carry, too. The last thing I needed was for her to convince the duke to take away my weapons again.

Mandy wore a faded jean jacket and a pair of her nicer

jeans. Werewolf or not, in her human form, she was petite. Even though her pair of TDs, tucked in the holsters under her arms, were the 9mm compact models, they pushed out the folds of her jacket. Hopefully, whatever getup Ethan was working on for her would be more concealing. I was already plotting how to get in touch with him before the final fitting to see if he could somehow incorporate pockets into the dress design that allowed me to reach my thigh holster.

"Here." Murphy nudged my shoulder with a pair of ear-muffs. "Just because we heal now doesn't mean we should be careless." He'd all but lost the hearing in his right ear as a human, so I wasn't surprised by his caution. These are the noise-filtering kind, so you'll be able to hear me even when they're on," he added.

"Why haven't you mentioned the range to me before now?" I asked, taking the muffs from him.

"You never asked." Murphy shrugged sheepishly. "Besides, I thought you already knew." His eyes slid to Mandy, and her nostrils flared with offense.

"Don't look at me!" she snapped. "I just got in trouble yesterday for telling Yosh we're flying to Denver. My lips are zipped."

"Is Yoshiko coming with us?" I asked, turning back to Murphy.

"No. She, uh… She's needed here to run the harem." He

popped his ear-muffs on and pulled one of his pistols, waiting for us to do the same.

The two wolves who had remained behind with us waited patiently in lanes at the far end of the room. Murphy slugged a button along the low wall of the first booth, and a small, mechanical arm latched on to one of the targets, hooking it over the first ceiling rail. I pulled my muffs on and hit the button inside my stall, following his lead the same as everyone else.

"I want to see your best for five, fifteen, and twenty-five—five shots each, from both hands. You're allowed two full runs," Murphy shouted. "And no dillydallying. Bad guys don't wait around for the next shot."

The rails whirred softly as they dragged the targets out to the first mark of five yards. I drew the TD on my right side with my left hand first. After training at the bat cave, I was pretty accurate with both, but some time had passed since then, so I stuck with my dominant hand.

"Going hot!" Murphy shouted, giving the go-ahead.

The ear-muffs clicked as the first shot sounded, dropping the volume to a comfortable level. I lined up my sights and ripped off five shots, trying to keep up with the others. No need to give them any more reason to doubt me. I could be a duchess and a badass all in one. I'd show them.

My aim wasn't perfectly center, but I didn't miss the

target. I pressed the button to reel in the silhouette and rolled it up before stuffing it down into a bin inside the booth as I'd watched Mandy do. Then I sent out another sheet and kept going, determined not to be the last to finish.

Halfway through the session, after we'd completed the first round and emptied the magazines in all our pistols, we broke to reload. Several boxes of Silver Wolfsbane target ammo were stashed on a shelf under the small stretch of counter that separated my booth from the shooting lanes. I ejected my magazines and set the TDs down before digging one of the boxes out.

"Yoshiko told me that she came from the Blood Okiya in L.A.," I said, glancing up at Murphy before I began reloading.

"Yeah, but she don't like to talk about it."

"I gathered that. Still, pretty damn impressive."

Murphy rubbed his knuckles under his chin and along his jaw, scratching the line of stubble there. There was pride in his smile, though he tried to hide it. "She's one of a kind."

In the booth on the other side of mine, Mandy swore as she pinched her finger in one of her magazines. When she realized that she was bleeding, she blew out an exasperated sigh and rolled her eyes. The sight of her blood made my tongue go dry.

"Is it snack time?" I asked, giving her an apologetic grin when she glared at me.

Mandy stuffed her hand down into the pocket of her jean jacket and dropped a handful of random junk on the counter between her pistols. She plucked a wad of tissue out of the mess and squeezed it around her finger before stuffing the rest of her loot back into the jacket pocket, pausing on a delicate, white gold charm bracelet. Tiny bats, coffins, and crowns dangled from the chain.

"The fuck?" she said under her breath as she examined it.

"That's new," I said, nodding at the jewelry. "It's pretty."

"It's not mine." She frowned. "I must have accidentally picked it up in the harem. I doubt it belongs to any of the guards." She shrugged and stuffed it back into her pocket. "Yosh will know. I'll drop it off to her later."

We finished reloading and began the second round. With each shot I fired, I felt the tension I'd been carrying around between my shoulder blades release a little more. I'd needed this more than I realized. Being cooped up in the manor with nothing more worthwhile than soap operas, etiquette lessons, and sparring to pass the time, my self-worth had taken a nosedive.

My mood lightened again once I finished and heard someone else fire off two last rounds. After the sheets had been examined, and we were all deemed acceptable shots, Murphy shouted, "Haulette! Our Slow Draw McGraw. You get to clean up the casings."

"Aw, man," the guard grumbled, but he set to work as Murphy led the rest of us out of the range room and back down the long hall toward the stairs.

I let Mandy and the other guard go up ahead of me so I could thank Murphy one more time.

"Don't mention it," he said, almost as if it were a request.

I nodded in understanding, silently vowing to keep the meeting and range session to myself. It didn't seem like that would be hard to do, what with the duke and me avoiding each other. I questioned that line of reasoning as I topped the stairs and entered the foyer.

Haunting music filled my ears and froze my heart.

Chapter Twelve

A white baby grand piano rested in the corner of the foyer near the entrance. Audrey sat in front of it, her fingers dancing lightly over the keys while Dante stood off to one side, his eyes closed and a blissful expression on his face.

Between that look and the heartbreaking melody, a lump formed in my throat. This was a siren's song, and if I weren't careful, I was sure I'd be dashed against the rocks of some unforgiving shore. But before I could decide whether or not slipping by unnoticed was even an option, the song ended, and Dante clapped his hands.

"Wonderful!" He sighed and touched Audrey's shoulder, bringing a flush to her cheeks. She turned a deeper shade of red when her gaze snagged on me. Dante turned around to see what had caught her attention. "Ms. Skye!" He sounded surprised. "I didn't see you there."

"Oh? Well, I didn't see you either," I said, feeling foolish for the comment before I'd even finished speaking. "I just heard the tail-end of the song…"

"She's very good, isn't she?" he said, smiling down at Audrey.

"Wonderful," I repeated his earlier praise. "Darkly does them right, huh?"

Audrey twisted her fingers in the lap of her frilly dress.

Then she glanced up at the wall above the piano, and I noticed the portrait of Ursula.

"You're rather talented yourself," she said, offering the compliment with a timid smile.

"Yes," Dante echoed. "The princess was quite proud of your rendering. She insisted that it be hung somewhere everyone could enjoy it."

"Speaking of the princess," I said, seizing the opening, "I have a lesson to prepare for. If you'll excuse me, Your Grace. Audrey." I mentally patted myself on the back for acknowledging the girl without making a face.

"Please," Dante said as I headed for the south wing. "Allow me to walk you to your room. We have not spoken in some time. I would very much like to catch up." He looked down at Audrey and touched her shoulder again. "I'll leave you to break in your new instrument."

Taking the cue, she smiled and went back to the keys, touching them softly as he crossed the foyer to join me. I swallowed and tried to smile at him, but my face wouldn't cooperate. How had things become so awkward between us in just a week?

"You're armed," he said after we'd walked a short way down the hall. "I've been a vampire for one hundred and fifty-three years," he added at my wide-eyed, guilty expression. "I can even smell the toothpaste you used earlier tonight. *Minty*."

He inhaled a deep breath.

"I just came from the basement range," I confessed, leaving Murphy's name out of it and ignoring the comment about my breath.

"Ah. I see." Dante nodded and folded his hands behind his back. "Is that what's been keeping you so busy this past week?"

"Maybe." I shot him a sideways glance. "What's your excuse?"

Dante made an affronted noise. "We acquired three new residents last week—one of which I intend to sire—and two others for the harem the week before that. There have been arrangements to make and fittings for the All Hallows' Eve ball—" He stopped suddenly and grabbed my hand, halting my powerwalk down the hall. "I am sorry. You are right, I should have made time for you."

I pulled my hand out of his grasp and took the few remaining steps to my bedroom door. Dante followed me inside, not even waiting for an invitation. I took off my blazer and tossed it on the dresser. My blood was boiling, but I couldn't tell if it was more from anger or longing.

"You know," I said, putting my hands on my hips as I faced him. "I'm a practical girl. I don't expect to be swept off my feet. But if you're ditching me in favor of your new Stepford blood bride—"

"Ms. Moore is not my blood bride, and I'm certainly not...*ditching* you." The phrase sounded odd coming from his lips, as if he didn't quite understand it. Before I could explain it further, he shook his head. "Practical or not, you deserve to be swept off your feet, Ms. Skye."

I rolled my eyes. "Oh, *great*. Let me guess, this is the part where you tell me that the right guy is out there, and I need only wait for him to come along and—"

Dante closed the distance between us in two strides. His mouth latched onto mine, stealing my surprised breath as his tongue traced my lower lip. One hand pressed into my lower back, and his other curled around my neck, under my ponytail. I melted against him, my useless hands groping his chest and shoulders.

When he finally broke the kiss, I was lightheaded and speechless.

"I intend to do the sweeping, Ms. Skye," he said against my mouth, lips grazing mine.

"Consider me swept." I panted softly, enjoying the smell of my toothpaste on his breath.

I waited for the familiar pang of guilt to ruin the moment, but I didn't have time to dwell on Roman this time.

A bloodcurdling scream echoed down the hallway outside my room, reaching into every nook and cranny of the manor. It struck my heart with a jolt of adrenaline as sharp and sudden as lightning.

Dante and I held our breaths and stared at one another a moment before the shock released us. Then he tore off out of the room with me hot on his heels, a pistol already in my hand. We rushed down the south wing toward the foyer as another scream ripped through the manor.

This one was deeper and full of despair. And it belonged to Murphy.

Chapter Thirteen

Yoshiko lay on her back at the bottom of the south stairwell, her neck twisted at an unnatural angle. There was a pool of blood near her head, but it wasn't hers. The spill began at the spout of an overturned teapot. Shards of ceramic were scattered across the hardwood floor, the ruins of what I imagined were once a pair of espresso cups.

Murphy knelt on his knees beside Yoshiko, his hands hovering over her body as if he were afraid to touch her. He made a helpless, mewling sound deep in his throat, and then abandoned protocol to clutch her limp body to his chest, dragging her hair through the spilt blood.

Half a dozen guards stood in the mouth of the foyer, and more were fast approaching. Mandy appeared with another wolf, both in sweats and coming from the north wing where I assumed they had been working out in the gym. Their confusion spiraled into shock, and then fearful sorrow at Murphy's open anguish. Mandy's bottom lip quivered, and she shook her head in disbelief.

I dropped my gun to my side and covered my mouth with my other hand, swallowing back a sob. Audrey was weeping enough for all of us. The duke's scion-to-be stood just inside the south wing, not ten feet from where Yoshiko had fallen. Her back quivered as she sucked in a ragged breath. She turned at the sound of our footsteps and rushed into Dante's open arms, burying her face against his chest.

"I was… I was playing the piano, and I heard a crash." She sniffled and eased away to look at him with her watery, Bambi eyes. "It's just awful."

"This wasn't an accident," Murphy said, his voice raw with grief. He held up Yoshiko's arm, revealing a pair of fresh scratches that began at her wrist. His eyes turned up to the staircase next, his fangs sliding free with a lethal hiss as he laid Yoshiko's lifeless body on the floor again.

"Murphy—" I began, but he was already off, climbing the stairs three at a time. "Shit!" I holstered my pistol and raced after him.

"Lock down the house," Dante shouted to the other guards as I disappeared up the stairs after Murphy.

Screams sounded from the harem lounge, and I ran faster, my own fangs extending from a stab of adrenaline. It wasn't until I reached the top floor that I realized the duke was right behind me. His eyes were dilated, fangs budding beneath his upper lip.

"Escort the donors to their rooms," he said. "I'll take care of Mr. Murphy."

I nodded, unable to speak between my fangs and the tightness in my chest.

One of Audrey's donors-in-waiting appeared first,

rushing for the stairs as Dante headed into the lounge. I grabbed her by the shoulders, drawing a squeak from her when she noticed my fangs.

"To your room," I hissed, redirecting her through the galley kitchen to the back hallway that housed the harem bedrooms. Two more donors charged in my direction but quickly changed course when they saw where I'd pointed the first. The rest had already filtered out of the lounge—all except for one.

Murphy had the man pinned to the floor in front of an overturned sofa. I recognized him as one of the newcomers Yoshiko had introduced as the Alaskan. His face was swollen and red, likely from his lungs being crushed flat by Murphy's weight.

"Did you do it?" Murphy screamed in the man's face. "Was it you?" The man gurgled and shook his head, unable to offer a more substantial reply without oxygen.

Dante took Murphy by the shoulders and heaved him upright and back a few steps as if he weighed no more than a Halloween prop. Murphy hissed and reached for the man still laid out on the floor, while I rushed across the room and dragged the donor to his feet, helping him to the back hallway and into his room.

"Mr. Murphy," Dante said, his voice loud but calm. "We will get to the bottom of this, but not in this manner. You will not terrorize my harem in your quest for vengeance."

Murphy jerked his shoulders out of the duke's grasp, but he didn't head for the hallway I guarded. Instead, he turned and placed his hands on the fireplace mantel that divided the wall of windows spanning the length of the room. I caught sight of his face in the reflection of the glass, his fathomless, black eyes and the rivers running from them.

He rested his head on the mantel between his hands and loosed a gut-wrenching wail.

Dante waited for the sound to die and the sobs to begin before he rested a hand on Murphy's back. He didn't say anything, just offered a comforting presence while Murphy's world finished imploding.

For all my wanting to help with a murder investigation, this was not how I'd anticipated it would come to pass. Not where I lived. Not with someone I consider a friend as the victim. And not with a whole lot of jack and shit to work with.

Since the security system was undergoing an upgrade, the cameras in the manor were down, and they would be for another hour at the very least. There were over forty donors upstairs at the time of Yoshiko's death—if my quick headcount was correct—and I didn't need Mandy to confirm that they would *all* smell like the harem manager. She drew their blood on a regular basis, spent time in their rooms, getting to know them on a level personal enough to play matchmaker with the vamps in the house.

Murphy was clearly devastated in the worst possible way, but Yoshiko's death affected everyone who lived at the manor. From the humans she considered her flock to the vampires she kept well fed. She was even friendly with the wolves—especially Mandy.

After Murphy had finished crying his eyes out, Dante asked me to accompany his top guard downstairs and requested that I track down Ursula and Belinda while he addressed the donors. I didn't remember seeing his assistant or the princess in the foyer. Of course, Belinda's office and the library, where Ursula spent much of her time, were in the north wing so it would have taken them longer to reach the scene.

Murphy and I found them both downstairs with Audrey, lingering around the spot where Yoshiko had fallen. One of the guards was collecting a sample of the blood from the floor with several evidence swabs.

"Where is she?" Murphy rasped, his calm on the verge of shattering again.

"Downstairs," the guard answered. "The harem produce cellar. It's the coldest room in the house—the best we can do until…other arrangements are made."

Murphy swallowed and nodded as another guard began cleaning the remaining blood on the floor.

"What has happened, my scion?" Ursula demanded. "Was this an unfortunate accident or an assassination? No one is giving me a straight answer."

"She was murdered." Murphy's fangs began to lengthen again, and I squeezed his shoulder.

"All of the donors who were upstairs are in their rooms now," I said. "We'll question them until we get to the bottom of this. In the meantime, the house is on lockdown."

Murphy blinked stiffly, coming out of his daze long enough to bark a few orders at the guards. "I want two men on this stairwell and two on the north. If any of the donors try to make a run for it, I want to know right away."

"Yes, sir," the guards gathered in the south wing answered.

"The duke asked me to find you," I said, eyeing Ursula and Belinda. "Maybe we should wait for him in his room."

Audrey took a step toward me in silent inquiry.

"Oh. You, too. I guess." I turned and followed Murphy through the foyer and down the back hallway to Dante's room. Ursula, Belinda, and Audrey filed inside behind us. The duke's bedroom was the largest in the house, but it suddenly felt cramped.

Murphy dropped into one of the armchairs in front of the fireplace and stared absently at the floor. I was certain the duke wouldn't allow him to question the donors—not after the scare he'd given them, and not while he was so emotionally unstable. But I supposed keeping him in the loop was the best way to keep an eye on him.

"This is a disaster." Ursula huffed and plopped down on the edge of Dante's bed. "And I'm starving. Why does stress always make me so hungry?"

Audrey sucked her bottom lip and eyed the other side of the bed. Then her gaze slid to me, and she wisely took a seat on the bench pushed up against the footboard instead. Now was not the time to wonder if she was sleeping with Dante. The moment I'd shared with the duke was tarnished enough as it was.

Belinda dug her cell phone out of her pocket and punched in a number. "We need two pots of wolf blood delivered to the duke's room," she said into the receiver. "No, the harem is locked down, but there should be several tea service sets in one of the storerooms. Thank you."

"Thank *you*," I said once she ended the call.

"Don't thank me just yet." Belinda grimaced. "Security is already stretched thin with the system upgrade and the lockdown, and we'll be relying pretty heavily on those anemic, sleep-deprived wolves come sunrise."

"But the cameras should be working by then, right?" I asked.

She shrugged. "What will it matter if there's no one to watch them?"

"Surely *some* of the donors will be willing to give blood even if they're quarantined," Audrey said. "And I'm well enough to feed the duke again—" She bit her lip and shot me a nervous glance as if sensing the wrath that bubbled up in my chest. I did my best to ignore it, and her.

"We'll question the donors until sunrise," I said. "And again after sunset if that's what it takes."

Dante entered the room, and we all turned our heads toward him.

"Well…" He blew out a crestfallen sigh. "I believe we are in for a very long night."

Werewolf blood had been a good call on Belinda's part. One of the guards delivered it shortly after Dante's arrival. It soothed my nerves, and it seemed to calm Murphy's agitation, too. But it also made me feel guilty about the vamp guards who would have to go without until we came up with a plan.

Dante offered me the empty armchair in front of the fireplace, but I opted to sit on the bench at the foot of his bed. Beside Audrey. She'd scooted to one side as soon as he'd come into the room, and now that I was thinking clearly, I was more than happy to squash her cuddle party plans.

This was no time for her Darkly charms. It was also no time for my pettiness, but if I had to watch her fawn over Dante, there was no way I'd be able to focus on what needed to be done—for Murphy's sake and everyone else's.

"Belinda," Dante said, lifting his cup of blood at her in thanks before continuing. "I know I count on you for a lot, but I am putting you in charge of harem management until we find a suitable replacement."

Murphy snorted. "Good luck with that."

Dante gave him a guarded look. I wasn't used to the guards or staff showing any disrespect toward the duke—that seemed to be something he only tolerated from Ursula and me. "It will be difficult," Dante finally said. "And it is doubtful that we will find someone as proficient as Ms. Onishi was, but we must make do as well as we can."

Belinda nodded, and her fingernails clicked swiftly over the screen of her phone. "I have a list of donors who are handy in the kitchen and good at finding veins—Yoshiko left it with me when she took a weekend off over the summer. I know she kept a planner with the donor matches and dates, too."

"It's in her room," Murphy said. He sniffled and then

cleared his throat. "Top drawer of her desk. It has the chore schedule in there, too."

"Thank you." Belinda gave him a sympathetic smile. "You wouldn't happen to know where she wanted to take her…forever rest, would you?"

"Yosh was human. She wanted to be cremated and to have her ashes scattered over the lake out back."

Dante set his empty espresso cup down on the table between the armchairs. "We can certainly do that for her."

"Yeah?" Murphy snorted again. "You wanna do something for her, find the sorry fuck who did this."

"I fully intend to," Dante said. The lines of his face tightened again at Murphy's tone. "But we will go about the task with level heads—while *you* tend to Ms. Onishi's final requests." Murphy looked as if he might refuse, but then Dante added, "She would have wanted it to be you."

"Yes, Your Grace." Murphy stood and sighed heavily, his gaze veering for the door. "I should be with her now."

Dante nodded. "Go."

I waited for Murphy to leave the room before asking, "Where are we interrogating the donors?"

"*We*, Ms. Skye?" He gave me a hesitant frown.

"Belinda made a good point right before you joined us." I stood and crossed the room, stopping behind Murphy's vacated armchair. "The guards are stretched thin right now, and we really can't afford to overwork the wolves and then expect them to hold down the fort after sunrise."

"It's a setup!" Ursula wheezed in a tight breath, and then another, sounding as if she were on the verge of hyperventilating. She crawled across Dante's bed and dropped to the floor on the opposite side from the wall of windows. "It's Kassandra. She's trying to kill me again."

"Kassandra?" Audrey gasped. "The Duchess of House Lilith? Are you ill? Have you been poisoned?" She climbed off the bench and pressed her back against the armoire to get a better view of Ursula's act taking place behind the bed.

"She's fine," I said, rolling my eyes. The princess's dramatic outbursts had gotten stale for me, but I remembered my initial panic the first few months after Imbolc. "You'll get used to this shtick soon enough."

"You could at least *pretend* like you care," Ursula snapped, pausing her labored breathing long enough to scowl at me.

"You're a *vampire*. You can't *die* from a panic attack."

"My office," Dante said, heading off our familial bickering. "We'll question the donors there. Belinda, have one of the guards on the south stairwell bring them down one at a time."

"Yes, Your Grace." She lowered her phone and dipped her head in a small bow. "I'll have the guard fetch Yoshiko's planner while he's upstairs, too."

"W-what about me?" Audrey asked. "Is there something I can do to help?"

"It is late, my dear." Dante went to the armoire and took her by the elbow. "I will escort you to your room where you'll be quite safe," he added, shooting an unamused look down at Ursula where she sat on the floor.

"Would you…could you, perhaps, interview Kate and Polly first?" Audrey asked as Dante opened one of the double doors. "I'd feel much better if I knew they were safe in my room with me—especially if there's a murderer in the harem."

"Yes, of course," he said, ushering her into the hallway. Belinda slipped past him and joined her as Dante looked back at me. "I'll meet you in my office."

Chapter Fourteen

"Kate Tillman?" I asked, fingering through the file Belinda had left on Dante's desk.

The girl in the guest chair gave me a weak smile. She wasn't the one I'd bumped into at the top of the staircase during Murphy's meltdown, so I now guessed that had been Polly.

"Yes, ma'am—I mean, Your Grace." Kate's face flushed at the blunder, and she wrung her hands in her lap. The mannerism and her politeness reminded me of Audrey, and I wondered if it was a Darkly Hall influence that all their prodigies acquired.

I paced behind Dante's chair, not feeling brave enough to claim it. A single kiss didn't mean what was his was mine or vice versa. He was still the Duke of House Lilith, and even a fledgling duchess like me knew certain lines shouldn't be crossed.

"The duke will be here any minute," I said. "But I see no reason why we can't get started without him." I glanced up from the file, waiting for her to protest. When she didn't, I continued. "When was the last time you saw the duke's harem manager?"

Kate touched her fingertips to her chin and blinked a few times. "I believe it was just after dinner. She came to Polly's and my room to draw Polly's blood."

"The other donor from Darkly? Why would Yoshiko take her blood?" I asked.

Kate bit her lip—another Audrey mannerism that annoyed me. "Our mistress offered to take us to Denver with her to see the queen's estate, but she said we must donate blood to her future sire to secure a seat on the flight. I declined, but Polly agreed. The harem manager was collecting a small taste for the duke to sample."

I doubted that the blood pot found beside Yoshiko's body contained Polly's blood. Dinner was served in the harem before sunset so the donors would be ready for the vamps in the house as soon as they rose for the evening. The Polly sampler had probably been the duke's first meal of the night.

If Kate weren't bleeding—beverage-wise—and Polly had been drawn off earlier in the night, that left...thirty-eight donors to question. *Very long night, indeed.*

"Was Ms. Onishi acting differently than usual? Did she say anything that struck you as odd? Complain about anyone in the harem?" I said, falling back on the generic questions every detective knew to ask.

Kate gave a small shrug and cocked her head to one side. "I've only been here a week, so I'm afraid I wouldn't know about the way she usually behaves... She was nice, if that helps? And she didn't speak ill of anyone." Her brows knit together. I waited, thinking perhaps she remembered something useful, and then she asked, "Do donors go missing around here often? Are we…safe?"

"Missing?" I blinked at her. *Shit.* She didn't know. "Yoshiko is dead."

Kate gasped and covered her mouth with both hands. "Was it that guard?" she whispered. "The one Polly said attacked the harem?"

"What? No." I slashed my hand through the air. "He discovered her at the bottom of the south stairwell and was looking for the one responsible."

"So, there's a killer in the harem?" Her voice cracked, and she bunched the front of her skirt in her hands, anxiously kneading the material. "And you left us upstairs with them?"

The office doors opened, and Dante entered the room. He looked tired, but a neutral mask smoothed his features as he took in Kate's mounting panic.

"Ms. Tillman?" he said gently. "Are you all right?"

"No, I'm not all right!" She pinched her eyes shut. "You told the headmistress at Darkly that you would protect us from harm, and now there's a killer loose in the house?"

"We do not know that for certain." He shot me an accusing stare. "We are questioning everyone—"

"Wait, am I a suspect?" Kate gasped again, and I thought she might dissolve into an Ursula-esque meltdown. *Great.*

Another drama queen. That was just what we needed.

"You and thirty-nine other donors," I said dryly, earning another look from Dante.

"No one is a suspect yet," he assured her. "For all we know, this could have been a simple yet tragic accident."

"I overheard the princess accusing the new donor from Spain of being an assassin sent to kill her," Kate confessed. "And now the harem manager is dead… I want to go home. You can't keep me here against my will!" Kate covered her mouth, muffling a sob as tears gathered at the corners of her eyes.

"Of course not, my dear." Dante knelt beside her chair and touched her arm, retracting it when she flinched. "I will make the arrangements. You may stay with Audrey in the meantime. I will have one of the guards collect your personal belongings from the harem."

"Thank you, Your Grace." She sniffled and stood as Dante did, letting him walk her out—though he didn't try to touch her again.

In the foyer, I heard him exchange a few words with the guards, instructing one to escort Kate to Audrey's room and another to fetch Polly. Then he came back into the office and closed the doors before turning around and slumping against them.

"That could not have gone much worse," he said in a flat

tone.

I shrugged. "It probably won't get any better when Donnie shows up to swab her nails—he's digging out all the cotton swabs and sandwich bags we have in storage. We don't have enough evidence kits for all forty donors and can't exactly run out for more while we're on lockdown."

"I think we can safely skip the extra trauma for Ms. Tillman."

"Why?" I snorted. "Do they not teach theater at Darkly? Or do royal vamps develop a flawless bullshit detector on their one hundred and fiftieth birthday?"

Dante closed his eyes and squeezed the bridge of his nose. "I realize that you are not fond of the girls from Darkly Hall. I can appreciate your resentment, but I must ask that you refrain from intimidating them into fleeing."

"I wasn't *trying* to scare her off." I folded my arms and leaned against his desk. "And why should I resent her or anyone else from Darkly?"

"Ms. Skye, you are an open book." Dante sighed and gave me a patronizing smile. "Audrey has trained and prepared for this life, while it was thrust upon you. She is taking it in stride, bypassing most of the growing pains you have endured."

"Taking it in stride?" I scoffed. "So, all her screaming and squawking hysterics earlier, that's what you consider 'taking it in stride'?"

"We all grieve in our own way—"

"And that's not why I dislike Audrey," I snapped. "You know better than that."

He pushed away from the doors and walked to me, stopping a few inches away. "There are blood lovers, and there are blood children. I was to Alexander what Audrey will be to me."

I thought of the marks on her wrist, of the way she lit up at his every touch and compliment. "Does *she* know that?" I asked.

Dante nodded and eased in closer. "But I need you to know it."

A knock at the door broke our standoff, and Dante backed away before circling his desk. "Enter," he called.

The doors opened, and Polly was led into the room. Her face was a swollen mess of tears and snot that she dabbed at with a shredded wad of tissues. I snatched a few fresh ones from a box on Dante's desk and handed them to her, trying to hide my relief when she didn't offer me the spent ones to dispose of for her. Still, I played it safe and edged around the duke's desk, opting to stand beside his chair.

"Ms. Hughes," Dante began softly as Polly took the chair Kate had sat in moments before. "Do you recall the last time you saw Ms. Onishi, my harem manager?"

"She took…my blood…after dinner," Polly rasped in

between heaving breaths. Then she dissolved into a fit of sobs that I had to raise my voice to be heard over.

"Do you know who else's blood she was planning to draw tonight?"

"No," Polly wailed. "I don't know anything."

"Well, clearly you know *something*," I said under my breath. Dante shot me a warning glare. "What? Why else would she be carrying on like this?"

"That guard was so angry." Polly covered her face with both the new and old tissues. "I thought he was going to kill someone. *Did* he kill someone?"

"You were in the lounge. I saw you at the top of the stairs." I frowned at her. "But you didn't see Yoshiko come through with the blood?"

Polly shook her head and hiccupped. "I was watching a movie with the others. I heard a scream, and then the guard came upstairs and attacked Noah." She paused to sob. "Is Noah okay?"

"He's fine—maybe a little sore," I added, remembering the upturned sofa and the way Murphy had had the poor guy pinned to the floor. "Who else was in the lounge with you, watching the movie?"

Polly shook her head. "I...I don't have all of their names memorized yet. Hannah, maybe? Oh God, I don't know." The pitch of her voice spiked, threatening to degrade into a wail.

"That will be all, Ms. Hughes," Dante said. "I'll have one of the guards take you to Audrey's room where you can stay until we sort all of this out."

"Thank you," she sobbed, covering her face again.

After the duke had walked her out and spoke with the guards, we had another moment alone before the next donor was brought down.

"Please tell me whoever you requested next *isn't* from Darkly," I said, squeezing the back of my neck with one hand. The damsel in distress bawling was already grating on my nerves.

"I called for Noah," Dante said, giving me a tight smile that suggested he was getting tired of the waterworks, too. "We should confirm that he does not require medical attention, and perhaps he will be able to give us a better idea of who all was in the lounge at the time of Yoshiko's death."

"If they were watching a movie, like Kate said, it's doubtful anyone saw anything." A lump pushed its way up my throat. Dante touched my chin and then my arm, letting his fingers trail softly down my skin. I wanted to take comfort in him, but we had such a long way to go yet.

"I imagine whoever the culprit is will be hesitant to let us swab under their nails," he said, offering a morsel of hope. It also cued my brain to start working again.

"We need a guard stationed upstairs in the harem's private quarters, and we should pull roommates back to back, so Yoshiko's murderer doesn't get tipped off before we have a chance to collect a sample from them."

"Good thinking, Ms. Skye." The inner corners of his eyebrows curled upward, painting his face with the sympathetic light I was so drawn to. "Thank you for your help with this difficult matter. I am ever so grateful to have you by my side this night."

Another knock cut our moment short, and we parted to begin the interrogation process anew.

By some miracle, we made it through all forty donors with half an hour to spare before sunrise. And not a single damn one of them had seen anything or even flinched when we asked to swab under their nails. Most also cried their eyes out upon hearing about Yoshiko's death. Even the most recently recruited donors welled up at the news.

I left Dante's office feeling foolish and defeated. And hungry. It had been over six hours since we'd regrouped over the werewolf blood, but I didn't have it in me to complain. The guards had to be thirsty, too, and they'd gone without for longer than I had. Of course, I had bigger bats to fry.

I slipped down the back hallway to Dante's room to see how Ursula was faring. She'd deemed his room safer than her own for the time being, despite the obnoxious number of windows, and had remained behind with a half-full blood pot to keep her company. As my sire, I felt obligated to at least check on her.

All the lights in Dante's room were off except for the reading lamp on his bedside table. Ursula sat under its pale glow on the floor, in the same spot I'd left her. The black tights she wore blended into the shadows under Dante's bed, almost as if she'd been hiding under there and had just come out—for a refill on her blood, apparently.

The princess clutched a bloodstained espresso cup in one hand and a teapot in the other, pouring out the last of the blood. I was surprised there was any left at all. She didn't seem the type who understood the concept of rationing.

"Did you find the assassin?" she asked, her wild, blue eyes searching mine for answers.

"Not yet."

"Then what are you doing in here? Go do your job!" She chucked the empty blood pot at me. It landed at my feet and bounced off one of my ankles before skittering away. The lid popped open, and a trickle of blood trailed across the hardwood floor.

"Sunrise is in thirty minutes, and we're waiting for DNA

results from the lab," I said through clenched teeth. "Rest in peace, Your Highness." I threw my arm to one side for a mocking bow.

I expected Ursula to lob the espresso cup at me next, but it contained the last of her safe-room blood supply. She glared at me as she gulped it down, but I managed to slip out of Dante's room before she finished it. She'd have to leave her hidey-hole if she wanted to have a food fight.

The south wing was quiet. I slowed as I passed the stairwell. The blood had been cleaned from the floor, but the two wolf guards watching the stairs were a dark reminder of all that had happened tonight. I nodded to them before heading on toward my room.

My head ached. I pulled the elastic out of my hair and looped it over my wrist so I could massage my scalp with both hands. A bath sounded like a great idea, but there wasn't enough time. The sun was already quieting my bones, sapping the energy from my muscles. I needed to lie down.

I opened my bedroom door and was surprised to find the bed empty but the lights on.

"Ms. Starsgard's shift began an hour ago." Dante reclined in the chair at my drawing desk with one of my library books open in his hands. "I wondered what had happened to my copy of Ambrogio's poems," he said, flipping through the pages fondly. He paused and hummed to himself before reading aloud. "*You are sand, traveling across the lifeline of my ageless hand, gathering in the grooves of no woman's land.*"

I hugged myself. "Sounds like something Murphy should read over Yoshiko's ashes."

The duke nodded. "Indeed, he might."

"How's your pending blood daughter?" I asked, trying to take his words at face value.

"Audrey is quite distraught over Kate's plans to return to Austin."

I shrugged. "Ursula is distraught, well…because she's Ursula."

Dante laughed softly, then he closed the book of poetry and set it back on my desk, on top of the etiquette book on eye contact. "Would you like to go somewhere with me tomorrow night?" he asked.

I blinked at him. "You mean leave the manor?"

"Yes."

"Before solving Yoshiko's murder?"

He sighed. "I am beginning to doubt the nature of her death."

"But the scratches—"

"—could have been caused by any variety of things." Dante rested his elbows on his knees and dropped his face into his hands. "I have spoken with the forensics department at Blood Vice. The scratches are inconsistent with wounds caused by fingernails, and they contain no DNA other than Ms. Onishi's own. Which makes me certain that we will not find her DNA in any of the donors' swab results."

I raked a hand through my hair and turned my back to him, hiding my disappointment. He'd done everything he could—well, besides set fire to the manor with everyone in it. That seemed like the only way Murphy was going to get the justice he wanted for Yoshiko.

"But it's so soon after your potential scions were targeted. You're not even a *little* bit concerned that this could be somehow be related?"

Dante groaned out an exhausted sigh. "If I suspected every tragedy that befell me was part of some grand conspiracy, I would be cowering in a corner somewhere like our poor princess."

Maybe it *had* been just a tragic accident. Yoshiko could have lost her balance, misjudged a step on the stairs. Maybe House Lilith really was unlucky enough to suffer this much misfortune in such a short span of time. In which case, they could join the club. *Or*, I supposed, *I could join the family*.

"Does Murphy know about this yet?" I asked, moving on to our next impossible problem.

Dante sighed. "I will break the news to him after his return from the funeral home tomorrow, once he has had a chance to spread Ms. Onishi's ashes over the lake. And after we've returned from Chicago."

"Chicago?" I spun around to gape at him.

"As much as I sympathize with Mr. Murphy, this household has needs that cannot go unmet," the duke said. "You may think Ursula…*eccentric* at times, but she is not incorrect about needing to keep up appearances before our enemies. I suspect that is why she acts out so boldly amongst us, to *get it out of her system*, as the young humans say."

"What household need are we picking up in Chicago?" I asked, steering him back on track.

Dante stood and looped his fingers through the straps of my shoulder holster. It was a small, innocent gesture, but my heart reeled at his touch, at the full weight of his gaze. When he was this close, everything felt…*intimate.*

"We are down a donor-in-waiting for my scion-to-be," he said, breaking the spell I was under. I didn't want to talk about Audrey. I wanted his mouth on mine again. Maybe that would help distract me from the gloom saturating the air.

I groaned softly and leaned into him, hoping he would get the hint. His hands stayed on my shoulders though, fingers sliding up and down the holster straps.

"I would like you to come with me to pick out the replacement donor," Dante continued. "I trust your judgment. And your interviewing skills."

"My interviewing skills?" I smirked. "Right."

"Are you turning down my offer, Ms. Skye?"

"I didn't say that."

"Good." His breath danced along my cheek and caused me to hold my own for a beat as I waited for him to close the gap. His lips swept in, just barely grazing mine. Then his hands fell away from my shoulders. He retreated, slipping past the bed and me. "Be ready by 7:00 P.M. tonight."

I huffed out a frustrated sigh as he closed my bedroom door behind him.

Chapter Fifteen

I'd never been on a plane. It hadn't seemed like such a big deal before Tuesday night, but now I was questioning my lax approach.

Lane drove us to the small airport downtown where Dante kept his private jet and, moments later, we were rolling down the runway. The two guards who were accompanying us on the outing were already stretched out in the back of the plane, one reading a paperback, and the other watching a movie on a small flat screen.

Dante sat across the aisle from me, the picture of calm. He tilted his head and offered a placid smile as if he'd done this a thousand times. For all I knew, he had.

"This plane is as old as you are," he mused aloud.

"Is that supposed to be comforting?" I closed my eyes and tried to breathe through my nose, wondering if vampires were immune to motion sickness.

The sound of the jet as we gained momentum made my chest tighten. When the armrests on my seat groaned in protest, I realized that I was holding onto them for dear life. Dante's hand closed over mine and squeezed softly. I strained to hear him over the hum of the engines.

"I have the plane serviced regularly, though I only use it when time or security is of the essence," he said. "The wolf guards check it for signs of tampering or bombs before each liftoff. It is perfectly safe."

"Bombs?" I squeaked. "Remind me again why being royalty is so great?"

"Besides holding the highest level of respect—insincere as most of it is—and financial freedom?" he asked, giving me a thoughtful frown. "I suppose that depends on your definition of great."

The plane bounced over a bump on the runway. I clamped my knees together anxiously as we gained momentum and then sank deeper into my seat. Outside my window, the runway lights turned red. It seemed odd until I realized my panic had triggered the Eye of Blood. The lights blurred and slowly disappeared as we lifted off.

Dante squeezed my hand again, but I was too captivated by the darkness. And then the city appeared, defying the night. The Arch came into view, glowing brightly above the St. Louis skyline and reflecting off the river. The sight stole my breath.

We rose higher, and the city lights shrank below us. The force pressing me into my seat relented, and for a brief second, I felt weightless.

"I really should fly more often." Dante's voice sounded far away. I swallowed, and my ears popped.

"Ouch." I shook my head.

"I'd offer you some gum, but it would only upset your

stomach. But perhaps some blood will help."

A flight attendant appeared with a cart holding a carafe of dark blood and several coffee mugs.

"Refreshment?" she asked.

Dante nodded, and she lifted out a couple of glossy, wooden tables from the side walls of the plane, latching them into place before us. She filled a pair of mugs for Dante and me before moving on to the guards in back.

"Is this another adventure you intend to keep from Ursula?" I asked in between careful sips of blood. It was hotter than I expected, likely kept over a burner until served.

"It shouldn't be too difficult." Dante gave me a dry grin. "She's in one of her moods, and you know how those work. She will sulk in her room for the next night or so until the excitement in the manor dies down."

"Why don't you fly more?" I asked, circling back to his earlier comment.

"It is wasteful, for one." He snorted. "I suppose I do not have Ursula's same taste for excessive indulgence. There are also greenhouse gases and climate change to take into consideration. When you are immortal, the future of the planet becomes a bit more relevant. That is why House Lilith built wind farms in Colorado, Kansas, and Texas. It is how I ended up in St. Louis, the closest major city to the land where we intend to build our next wind farm, in Illinois."

Dante paused to smile at me. This was the most I'd heard him talk about the family business—if it even *was* the family business. There was a chance this was just one iron in House Lilith's fire. I didn't know how much information I was privy to as duchess now.

"Listen to me, boring you with all this business talk." Dante laughed and reached up as if to run his hand through his hair, remembering at the last moment that it was slicked into place with gel—part of his professional persona for the outside world.

"I don't mind," I said, setting my mug down on the table in front of me. "Though, I would like to know why we're picking up this replacement donor personally. You didn't do that with the others."

"And you see how well that turned out." Dante sighed and looked out his window. "It is difficult not to feel responsible for the deaths of those I previously chose."

"The first one might still be alive," I said, reaching across the aisle to take his hand this time.

"No." He turned and gave me a sad smile, rolling his thumb over my knuckles. "I do not wish to cause Ursula or Audrey any more distress, so please, keep this to yourself. Ingrid's body was found late last week."

"Oh. I'm sorry." I blinked at him, not sure what else to say.

He nodded, accepting the condolences. "All of the donors in my harem were made aware of the risk that comes with working for a member of the royal family—and the potential scions were even more informed. But this aggressive assault, that I have no doubt Kassandra is behind, has left me feeling raw. Vulnerable."

"What does she have to gain from this?" I wondered aloud.

I already had a pretty good idea of why she'd tried to have the queen assassinated. Lili was over four hundred years old, and she'd been ruling for over two hundred of those years. Like Lilith, her sire before her, she'd grown tired. Rumors that she would be taking her forever rest—a voluntary death of sorts for vampires that I equated to assisted suicide—had been circulating for some time.

When Lilith had taken her forever rest, she'd taken Adam, her firstborn scion and lover, with her. I didn't know the specifics, and I wasn't sure whom to even ask. Dante hadn't been alive at the time, and Ursula would have been a young, human girl in Vienna, under Mozart's spell.

I supposed Alexander, the prince, would have been there on the day Lilith and Adam said goodbye and Lili took the throne. Maybe it was his version of the big day that had motivated Kassandra to such extremes.

Dante had shared his suspicions with me before Ursula's

trial. Namely, how he thought Kassandra feared that Lili would take Alexander with her to the grave. If the queen were eliminated before she had the chance, the crown would pass to the prince, and then Kassandra could rule by his side. It made sense, but without evidence, throwing around accusations would only tip her off that we were on to her. It would just make the job of outing her that much more difficult.

"Do you suppose the prince suspects anything of Kassandra?" I slipped my hand out of Dante's to cradle my mug of blood, not sure I wanted to be touching him while I voiced my reservations about his sire. How could Alexander not know the devil he was living and sleeping with?

Dante pressed his lips together and folded his hands over the table in front of him. "I do not wish to think unkindly of my blood father, but I do know that he is still in love with this world and would very much like to remain in it. However, I also know that he is fiercely loyal to Lili. He would do anything she requested of him. *Anything*."

"Were they lovers at one time?"

"Briefly." Shame tinted Dante's face, and I saw how much it bothered him to be gossiping about his sire. "He spent thirty years in her harem, half-sired, before she turned him. A few years after that…the queen lost interest. She has always been fonder of her human companions than her vampiric lovers."

I thought of Roman and swallowed. "Did they share a lifeblood bond?"

"I don't know." Dante shook his head. "Alexander did not like to speak of the past. It was too painful for him."

"If the queen doesn't want him anymore…then why would Kassandra think she'd take him to her forever rest?"

"Lili no longer beds him, but she still considers him her closest adviser and confidant." Dante gave me a meaningful look. "And it is customary, especially among royal families, to create two scions for the specific purpose of taking one as a companion into the eternal darkness and leaving one behind to rule over *this* darkness." He threw a glance over his shoulder at the night sky beyond his window.

Well, *that* certainly hadn't been in any of the books I'd read recently.

The flight to Chicago took all of an hour, which seemed crazy considering the drive was over four and a half. I remembered going up to check out the planetarium with Collins for spring break our senior year of high school. Laura had gone to Party Cove at Lake of the Ozarks with a slew of her faux friends and then talked me into buying a box of pregnancy tests for her after we came home.

There was a car waiting for Dante and me when we landed. One of the guards opened the door to the back seat, and Dante ushered me in ahead of him. I'd worn a skirt and heels, determined not to be underdressed for the occasion, so scooching across the seat was awkward, especially while clasping the lapels of my blazer with one hand so it wouldn't gape and reveal the TDs I was packing. Guards or no guards, I would be holding my own if the need arose.

After my preview of Bathory House and my exposure to the finished product of Darkly Hall, I didn't think Renfield Academy could offer any surprises. I should have known better.

We headed east, away from the clamor and radiance of the city. Twenty minutes later, we stopped at a gated entrance surrounded by fenced pastures. I heard the muffled voice of the guard in the driver's seat announce us to someone speaking through an intercom. Then a buzz sounded. The gate opened, and we rolled past it, heading down a long drive that dipped and curled around hills and clusters of trees.

Buildings soon came into view, a barn and two larger, two-story structures that reminded me of the barracks at the bat cave, stark lighting and all. A group of men wearing sweats jogged around the buildings in formation, an older man leading the way with a whistle pinched between his lips.

"Is this an all-male school?" I asked Dante as the car turned off into a small lot beside the barn.

"They receive an occasional female applicant, but for the most part, yes."

"Interesting," I mused, leaning against the window to get a better look at the grounds. A pair of horses galloped through an adjoining pasture and up to the barn, a streak of black on their heels. The creature paused, and golden wolf eyes turned toward the car. "Do they receive many werewolf applicants?"

"Renfield Academy is one of very few schools who accept them," Dante said. "They will not do for a scion, but as donors, they are quite desirable. And many of the human alumni who are not fully turned are half-sired and contracted through Blood Vice like—" He paused and sucked in a cautious breath as I turned back to him.

"Like Agent Knight." I offered him a small, forgiving smile before changing the subject. "This doesn't look like the kind of place where they teach etiquette and fine arts. But you were willing to select a scion from here?"

"Blood Vice is one of Renfield's most generous patrons. What better way to nurture that relationship than by choosing one of their own to sire?"

I twisted in my seat and frowned at him. "So, what? You went down the list of places you wanted to improve business relations with? That's how you decided where to find your future scion?"

His eyes widened. "What is wrong with that method?"

"What *isn't* wrong with it?" I huffed. "You should have visited loads of schools and met with dozens of potential candidates. You're going to be stuck with this scion for a very long time—and they're going to be stuck with you."

Dante gave me an annoyed scowl. "I am following the queen's orders, and I have been nothing but gracious and adoring toward Audrey."

Well. I could agree with that much. When I didn't say anything, Dante went on, his voice growing increasingly defensive.

"I do not have time to sort through endless candidates— the queen expects me to present her with my chosen at the ball. Next Imbolc, I will turn Audrey. The royal family has been compromised, and there is no time for lengthier formalities. Our enemies will not wait for us to recover. Certainly not the enemy within our own house."

"And you're returning here and not to the other two schools because…?" I asked, changing the subject again. Arguing with Dante was even less fun than it had been before I decided I wanted him. He sighed and gave me a look that suggested he felt the same.

"Bathory House was disappointed that I chose my second candidate from a different school, but after their pupils' brutalized remains were found, they are now seemingly *out of service*. Same for Darkly Hall after Ms. Tillman spoke with them." His shoulders sagged, and the hurt in his expression tore at my heart.

"What happened to them is not your fault," I said, reaching for his hand where it lay on the seat, but he pulled away before I touched him.

"I am not surprised, nor do I blame them." The serene mask he wore for the outside world slipped over his features once again. He straightened his vest as one of the guards exited the car and opened the back door.

"Your Grace," a bald man in dark fatigues greeted Dante. The man's confidence and massive build reminded me of Kai Natani, but his smile lacked the BATC instructor's self-satisfied humor. I bit my tongue, inflicting just enough discomfort to trigger my blood vision.

Human. No, *half-sired*, I decided after his pale eyes turned on me. I climbed out of the car behind Dante, wobbling on my heels in the gravel.

"Dr. Marquis, dean of Renfield Academy." The man held out his hand, taking mine in a firm shake. "You must be the future baroness—"

"This is the princess's new scion, the duchess tempus, Jenna Skye," Dante explained. "She's assisting me today."

Dr. Marquis' eyebrows rose, but he didn't say anything

more on the matter. Instead, he dipped his head in a polite nod before turning to lead us across the lot and into the nearest building. We bypassed an empty front desk and then wove through several hallways until we reached a conference room. A grouping of files was laid out on the long table.

"I have five candidates who meet your requested qualifications," Dr. Marquis said. "Take your time. I'll be in my office across the hall if you have any questions."

After he'd left us, closing the door behind him, I turned to Dante. "Friendly fella, ain't he?"

"I am lucky he has not turned me away like the others." Dante sighed and gave me a tightlipped smile that didn't reach his eyes. "The trainees here undergo a pre-boot camp of sorts, anticipating a career in Blood Vice. The school's reputation will suffer when news of their late student spreads. This is an opportunity for them to show that they are not discouraged by the royal family's enemies. Of course," —he eyed the files on the table— "there are fewer volunteers this time."

"What were your requested qualifications?" I asked.

"The usual." He flipped open a folder and removed a photo paperclipped to the inside flap. "No disciplinary issues, exceptional physical condition, loyalty under duress, no human family to complicate our already complicated household."

"And only five students qualified?" I asked, accepting the

photo from him.

"They are made aware of the house soliciting them and are free to submit or omit their name," Dante said. "Before one of their classmates died, there were dozens of files to choose from."

The photo of the first new candidate rubbed me wrong. He looked *smug*, his smile almost a dare for someone to cross him. House Lilith didn't need any help in that department.

I glanced over Dante's shoulder as he thumbed through the boy's file—the results of his most recent physical exam and psych evaluation, a birth certificate, FBI background check. He met the duke's requirements, but only just.

I discarded the photograph on the table and reached for another file, skimming through it and then a third before Dante had finished with the first. It was the fourth one that finally sparked my interest. His expression held more respect—an easy smile and warm, caramel-colored eyes—but it was the two extra letters of recommendation from instructors that really caught my attention.

"Try him," I said, dropping the kid's folder on top of the one Dante was reviewing.

"Levi Bishop—a wolf?" Dante gave me a hesitant look.

"They're harder to kill and more satisfying, donor-wise. It's been a while for you, but I know just how unbearable vampling thirst can be. Until Audrey gets comfortable with the process, every drop counts. If you don't want another diva around the manor, I suggest you feed her like you mean it."

"Hmm." He picked up the file and thoughtfully ran a hand over his chin. "This is your final choice?"

"That's just my two cents," I said, shrugging. "It's not my choice to make."

"But it is." Dante looked up from the file. "That is why you are here. Until Ursula is more…stable, it is my responsibility to integrate you into this family. That is why the queen put you under my roof. I want you to feel a part of the household. I want you to choose and welcome the next member."

I imagined this was some sort of warped apology for not realizing how much Audrey's presence would affect me. Or maybe it was Dante's way of distracting me from my desire to get out of the manor and work with Blood Vice.

I knew how tied his hands were. The queen would skin him alive if anything happened to me—or Ursula—and he was already risking the princess's wrath by sneaking me out of the manor for this short business trip. But somewhere in the last few months, the scales had tipped, and he was showing more interest in my happiness. If only I could get him to dial down his concern for my safety.

Dante's hand ran across my lower back. It was a casual gesture, but it rallied the butterflies in my stomach, sending them aflutter.

"I am leaving this choice to you, Jenna," he said, mistaking my silence for confusion.

"In that case…" I said, picking up the fifth file. "Better safe than sorry." I gave him a sheepish grin and opened the last folder.

Chapter Sixteen

Levi Bishop, the only wolf who had been in the running to be Audrey's new donor-in-waiting and my final choice, was a sweet kid from Tennessee. His parents had died in a car crash when he was ten. He spent a year in foster care until a playdate with a werewolf pup got a little out of hand.

The other kid's mom reported the incident, and then Levi was shipped off to Renfield Academy before he even hit puberty and had his first shift. From his psych eval, it didn't seem as though he held either accident against anyone. He had a very shit-happens attitude about life, and he seemed content to at least have a general idea of where his future was headed.

I'd grilled him on all kinds of random things on the flight back to St. Louis. Partly to get a better handle on his personality, but mostly to hear him talk. Seven years in Chicago at Renfield hadn't killed his Tennessee accent. It was thicker than Audrey's Texas drawl, but I had a feeling she wouldn't mind.

The few questions Dante asked were more invasive than mine.

Have you ever been bitten by a vampire? What factors solidify your loyalty? Do you aspire to join Blood Vice? Are you a virgin?

I wondered if he'd asked the same of Audrey and the other girls from Darkly Hall and Bathory House. I assumed he'd at least skipped the Blood Vice question. And the virginity one was probably a little too pearl-clutching to risk. Maybe I'd drop that one on *him* later and see what kind of reaction it earned.

When we arrived back at the manor, Dante headed straight for his office. "Belinda should have your room ready upstairs," he said, pausing at the double doors. "After the duchess gives you the tour, please, make yourself at home."

"Thank you, Your Grace," Levi said in his slow drawl and tugged the straps of his duffel bag higher up on his shoulder. "I appreciate the warm welcome," he added, almost under his breath as he took in the stone-faced guards standing to either side of the office doors.

"Hey, let's start with the gym," I suggested, nudging him toward the north wing. When he yawned, I added, "We'll save the library for tomorrow, let you get some rest first."

It was doubtful that Ursula had made it that far from her room tonight, but I was more than happy not to risk a run-in.

"What do the wolf folk around here do for the full moon?" Levi asked after we'd passed a second pair of humorless guards watching the north stairwell.

"Shit. That's tomorrow, isn't it?"

"Yep." Levi nodded.

I'd been paying better attention to the lunar cycles lately since Mandy planned her camping trips around the full moons. But none of the wolves were going camping this week. Not with the harem needing so much supervision during the day while the vamps were out of commission. They'd likely shift out back and prowl around the lake and trees on Dante's property, but then they'd have to call it quits earlier than usual so they wouldn't be too tired for their daytime shifts.

Even if Yoshiko's death were an accident, Dante would not have an easy time convincing Murphy. But, at some point soon, he would have to let up on the excessive guard presence. Either that, or hire more security—and maybe more donors if any of the current harem members decided they wanted to leave. If Murphy would *let* them leave without a full-blown apocalypse.

"I'll introduce you to Mandy tomorrow," I told Levi. "She'll be able to fill you in on the camping schedule for the local Cadaver Dogs she likes to hit the state parks with. I imagine Belinda, the duke's assistant, will have a household duty or two for you, but not for a few days. Our harem manager...had an accident, and things have been a little off around here lately."

"I just heard about the dowry donor quitting," Levi said, giving me an apologetic smile. "Harem management wasn't my strongest class at the academy—and they only train us on the basics of blood rationing for emergency situations."

I squeezed his shoulder as we stopped in front of the door to the gym. "Don't sweat it. Belinda knows what she's doing. I'm sure she'll have a new manager in place by the weekend."

The gym door opened, and Murphy stopped just shy of running us over. "Skye," he said, breath panting. Sweat soaked his hair and shirt. I glanced down at his hands, my eyes catching on the bloodied tape wrapped around his knuckles.

"Murphy." I did a double-take at his face, but it was fine—other than the flushed cheeks and film of perspiration. The heavy bag hanging in the gym behind him hadn't been so lucky. "I didn't think you'd be back until later…"

He ran an arm under his nose, wiping away a drop of sweat, and sniffled. "I couldn't sit there and watch her burn through a tiny window for three hours. There's too much that needs to be done around here. Who's this?" he asked, jerking his chin at Levi.

"Levi Bishop, sir," Levi introduced himself, holding out his hand before noticing Murphy's busted knuckles. "I'm the future baroness's replacement donor."

Murphy snorted and glared at Levi's hand before shooting me a wounded scowl. "I've worked here for thirty years. Yosh has been here for fifteen. The boss just picked his pending scion out of a catalog last week. She's not even turned yet, but replacing one of her blood dolls is more important than finding who killed Yosh?"

BLOOD, SWEAT, & TEARS | 161

"Killed?" Levi interjected. "I thought you said she had an accident."

Murphy blew out a trembling sigh, his eyes not leaving mine. "Is that so? Take you all day to decide that?"

"Didn't anyone give you the swab results when you got back?" I asked, wanting to touch his shoulder in comfort but too afraid of the intensity in his gaze.

"They could have washed their hands," he said. "They could have slipped around to the north wing before I made it upstairs. Those swabs don't mean shit."

"We interviewed all the donors last night, and the coroner said that the scratches were inconsistent with marks left by fingernails. What more can we do, Murph?"

"Let *me* talk to them," he said through clenched teeth. "I'll find the bastard responsible."

"Yeah, and scare the rest of the harem shitless in the process. How many donors do you suppose are ready to quit over last night's events as it is?" I folded my arms and tried to leave things at that. Murphy was hurting and probably thirsty. I wondered if Belinda had worked out a temporary system with the donors yet.

Murphy made a disgusted face at Levi again. "Does it matter? There are always more desperate humans ready to serve House Lilith despite the risk involved."

"Not human, buddy," Levi said, a low warning in his

tone.

"Dante's in his office." I moved aside so Murphy could pass between us. I didn't want to hear anything else he had to say. It was…uncomfortable, listening to him being so heartless about humans when Yoshiko had been one. I had to believe I knew him better than that. "We just got back from Chicago. I'm sure he'll want to speak with you."

"Right away, Your Grace." He snorted again and shook his head before stalking off down the north wing.

Levi blew out a tense breath. "They told us things might be complicated at the duke's house, but damn. I just thought one of the dowry donors quit after she found out what happened to the others, and the duke needed someone with a little more steel in their spine to replace her."

"That sounds about right." I led Levi inside the gym, where we could now see the other two hanging punching bags, both just as destroyed as the first and smeared with Murphy's blood. "So, this is the gym."

"It sure is." Levi whistled softly. "Good thing your pal prefers beating on the bags."

"He usually spars with me," I said, then groaned at Levi's slack-jawed surprise. "I was Blood Vice before the princess adopted me."

"I'd heard that," he confessed. "But I don't go around betting the farm on gossip, ma'am."

I nodded, deciding that was solid enough advice.

We left the gym and headed back toward the foyer, quickly cutting across to the south wing. I didn't hear shouting coming from Dante's office. I wanted to take that as a good sign, but I had a feeling it just meant that Murphy went to clean himself up first.

Levi's frown deepened as we passed the third set of guards on the south stairwell. "Are the donors restricted to the upstairs harem?" Levi asked, tugging up the straps of his bag again and glancing back over his shoulder.

"Not usually." I gave him a strained smile. "You're certainly not. I'm sure soon after the duke speaks with Murphy, the lockdown will be over. In fact, you can sleep in Mandy's room tonight if you want. She sleeps in my bedroom most of the time anyway."

He gave me an odd look but didn't say anything. We stopped in front of Audrey's room, and I rapped my knuckles on the closed door. Polly answered, peeking timidly out into the hall.

"Special delivery," I called, hoping Audrey wasn't asleep. I needed her to entertain Levi for a few minutes while I checked in on Mandy to make sure she wouldn't mind me loaning out her bed for a night.

"Your Grace. Please, come in." Polly curtseyed as she opened the door wider, revealing Audrey curled up in a chair along the far wall, eating chocolate truffles out of a box and watching *Henry's Courtroom*, of all shows. When she realized she had company, she hit pause, freezing the image of Laura leaning over Judge Henry's desk.

Levi gawked at the flat screen and then back at me as we entered the room. "Now, how do I hear about you being in Blood Vice but not that you were a movie star?"

"I'm not." My face flushed, and I waved my hand at the television. "Could you pause that on something other than my sister's tits. *Please.* For the love of all things holy."

"Sorry! Sorry." Audrey giggled nervously and fumbled with the remote until she'd walked Laura backward through the judge's door with the reverse button. "I—Yoshiko mentioned you had a famous twin sister—I just had to see for myself. The resemblance is striking."

"This is Levi Bishop," I blurted, eager to redirect the conversation. "He's Kate's replacement, and he's a werewolf."

"Nice to meet you, Miss Audrey." Levi held out his palm, and Audrey took it, blushing when he turned her hand up to kiss her knuckles. "My daddy taught me that a girl's hand should always be kissed when she's wearin' a pretty dress."

"Your daddy sounds like a smart man," Audrey cooed.

Levi nodded. "He sure was."

Audrey stared dreamily at him, folding her opposite hand

over the back of his, still wrapped around her dainty fingers. She batted her lashes and sighed. Levi seemed a little smitten himself.

"Maybe you have some questions for him?" I prompted Audrey. "Or some things to share about the manor while I check in on Mandy and let Dante know Levi will be sleeping in her room tonight."

"He will?" she asked, her breath hitching excitedly. "Oh! Questions, of course," she said, latching on to the more relevant part of my statement. She released Levi's hand so she could walk me to the door, while Levi wandered over to introduce himself to Polly.

"Is this a trick?" Audrey asked under her breath as I stepped out into the hallway. "You're being nice to me, and I like it, but I don't know if I can trust it."

"You're not sleeping with Dante."

"No, of course not," she whispered, shooting an embarrassed glance over her shoulder toward the window where Levi stood, peeking through the curtains out at the darkened front lawn.

"It wasn't a question," I said, giving her a tight smile. "And as long as you remember that, I'll play nice. We might even become friends—eventually."

Audrey looked over her shoulder at Levi again. "What about him? Is he off-limits, too?"

"Just wait until after Imbolc." If she went and got herself turned into a wolf before Dante turned her, I'd never hear the end of it. "*Please*," I added when her eyes lingered on Levi a little longer than was proper for an alumna of Darkly Hall.

"Okay, okay," she whispered, turning back to me. "I've spent the past eight years in an all-girls school, you realize. And now I'm in a house full of dozens of men—Adonises, the lot of 'em. My God, how do you do it?"

"Easy. I've only got eyes for one." The words felt like the truth in my mouth, but I doubted them the second they were uttered.

Was Dante the only one I had eyes for? Was I truly ready to close that door on Roman for good? Had our lifeblood bond finally faded? Was this thing I felt for Dante the real deal, rather than just a side effect of a few heady blood cocktails?

There was no easy answer. I felt my heart begging for a chorus of *yes, yes, yes*. Or maybe that was just my libido. But even with the two of them plotting against my reluctance, my conscience resisted.

I craved certainty, and it was in short supply.

Chapter Seventeen

Now that Mandy was working guard shifts for the house, being a wolf meant that she was swinging double shifts during the harem lockdown. It was probably for the best, giving her something constructive to do as she worked through the pain of losing Yoshiko, the closest new friend she'd made at the manor. Mandy was a lot like me in that respect, throwing herself into a task when grief was too much to bear. She'd set it aside to wallow in at a later date, putting on a poker face for the rest of the world.

I paused at my bedroom, hesitant to disturb her even though I was sure I wouldn't find her asleep. I sighed and rested my forehead against the closed door, taking a few deep breaths before I went inside.

The fire hydrant lamp on the bedside table filled the room with a soft glow, illuminating Mandy's backside where she lay curled atop the bedspread. Her bony spine peeked above the collar of her tank top, straining against her skin with each breath she heaved.

"He can have my bed," she whispered without me having to ask. Her wolfy ears were sharp. Too bad she'd been in the gym when Yoshiko had died. Maybe she would have heard if there had been an altercation between Yoshiko and one of the donors. I was sure she'd thought the same thing a hundred times already, so I kept the useless wish to myself.

"Thanks." I sat on the edge of the bed opposite her side.

"Belinda asked if I'd feed you before sunrise." Mandy sniffled and cleared her throat, but she didn't roll over. "My shift starts at six."

"I'll be here by five—with breakfast," I said, touching her shoulder. Her breath shuddered out in a long sigh, echoed by my own. "I'm so sorry, Mandy."

"Don't feel sorry for me." She sniffled again. "Murphy is the one you need to worry about. He's coming unraveled fast. The duke better do something about him before he loses his shit."

"Yeah." I swallowed and rested my elbows on my knees before dropping my face into my hands.

The problems I'd been whining about the week before seemed like a distant memory. I felt petty and selfish. Pining over Dante through all of this made me feel even more shameful.

I'd seen a therapist enough times after my mother's death to know that this was a normal part of grief—feeling undeserving of any shred of happiness. But knowing and accepting were two different things. I'd still cut myself off from so much for so long, devoting years of my life to honoring my mom's memory by retracing her steps. Until the path had ended, and I'd found myself here.

"You don't have to stay," Mandy said, curling herself into a tighter ball. "I'll be fine. I'm just going to close my eyes for a bit."

"Okay." I sat up and gave her shoulder another squeeze before sliding off the bed.

I closed the door softly behind me as I stepped back out into the hallway. Audrey's door was still closed, and I could hear her and Levi's muffled voices on the other side, deep in animated discussion. I decided to give them more time and went to check in with Dante first. If Murphy had made it to the duke's office, they were probably both in need of some moral support about now. And maybe a mediator. Whatever good it would do.

When I reached the south stairwell, Lane, one of the duke's most trusted guards who had accompanied us to Ursula's trial, nodded to me from his post at the foot of the steps.

"Any word on when this lockdown will be over?" he asked, ignoring the horror-struck look on his partner's face. Now that I was a duchess, the guards I hadn't gotten chummy with before were even less inclined to socialize with me.

"Soon, I hope." My gaze slid up the long staircase, and I couldn't help but picture Yoshiko's fall. "Has anyone tried to slip past you guys?"

Lane shook his head. "Belinda's keeping them busy with

preparations for a memorial. She says she should have a temporary blood schedule in place before sunrise, too."

"Have you seen Murphy tonight?" I pressed my lips together, wondering how aware the rest of the security staff was about their supervisor's mental stability. Lane shot his partner a nervous glance and then looked down at his feet.

"Donnie is filling in for him for the next couple of days," he said.

"Good."

It wasn't really an answer to the question I'd asked, but I let it go, knowing Lane likely didn't want to reveal the condition he'd found Murphy in. I hugged myself, letting my stare drop to the floor with Lane's gaze in silent sympathy for our mutual friend.

Everything was going to hell, and I felt useless. Some things just couldn't be fixed, and I was no longer in a position to help with any of the things that could be. Anxiety welled in my chest, and the Eye of Blood responded by bleeding pink all over my vision.

As my gaze pulled up, something small and shiny caught my eye, tucked in the shadows of the corner that wrapped around the side of the stairwell. Lane turned to watch as I slipped past the bannister to collect the trinket before my blood vision faded.

"Have either of Audrey's donors been up to the harem

since the lockdown?" I asked, a worm of doubt coiling in my chest.

"Not tonight." Lane shook his head and then looked to his partner who repeated the gesture. "The one who quit was picked up by a cab this morning before sunrise."

"Keep up the good work," I called over my shoulder as I headed past them and into the foyer.

One of the guards stationed outside the duke's office knocked for me before I'd even reached the double doors. Before attaining my duchess status, they questioned my reasons for approaching the duke, sometimes turning me away if they thought he was too busy to address whatever trivialities I could possibly think to bother him with.

"Enter," Dante called from inside the room. The guards opened the doors for me, immediately closing them once I'd passed through.

"Has Murphy come to see you yet?" I asked, scanning the room for any signs of blood or chaos.

"No, he has not." Dante frowned and set aside the stack of mail he'd been sorting through. "Though, I was informed that he had returned from the funeral home early. Have you seen him?"

I sighed, hating to add to Dante's overflowing plate of worries. "He's not doing so great."

Dante nodded, unsurprised. "What is that?" he asked

next, noting my closed fist. I held the bracelet up so he could get a better view of the dangling charms—bats, coffins, and crowns.

"Look familiar?"

He blinked and cocked his head to one side. "I believe that belongs to Polly, Audrey's remaining donor. Perhaps the clasp needs to be repaired—she loses the thing constantly."

"Does she?" I asked, letting Ursula's—and now Murphy's—paranoia summon up a dozen *what-if* scenarios. "I found it near the south stairwell."

"That *is* where her mistress's room is located, and where she has been staying since the lockdown," Dante reminded me. Still, doubt clawed at my mind, throbbing anxiously against my temples, as if there were something more—something I was missing.

"Is the tech team who updated the security system still here?"

Dante nodded. "They are still fine-tuning the new sensors. A slamming toilet lid should not initiate the alarms." He sighed and rubbed his forehead with his fingertips. "I cannot decide if it is a blessing or a curse that we are able to sleep through such events."

"Downstairs?" I asked, holding the bracelet up for closer inspection.

"Across from Mr. Murphy's office." Dante drummed his

fingers over his desk anxiously. "You realize that you are placing suspicion upon a teenage girl who was trained to be a submissive, companionable donor and not an assassin, yes?"

"Scarlett was a young, innocent-seeming creature," I replied. "And Mandy, as much as I love her, is perfectly capable of eating someone's face off if they cross her."

"But...Polly is a mere human," Dante argued. I clutched the bracelet and stared at him, deciding that maybe a healthy dose of paranoia was better than none at all.

"We all were, once upon a time."

The tech team Dante had hired to update the security system consisted of a wolf and a half-sired geek squad. When I poked my head inside the control room, I found them crammed in alongside four of the vamp house guards, showing them different features on the video feed screens.

"Could I borrow one of you for a minute?" I asked, drawing the half-sired tech's attention. She stood and met me in the doorway, shooting her colleague a strained smile.

"What can I help you with, Your Grace?"

I blinked at her, surprised she even knew who I was. Of course, if she knew that much, I could guess why she was so tense around me. Having a reputation for sticking my fangs into people they didn't belong in was not the most respectable way to make my debut as a vamp.

"Could you take a look at this?" I asked, handing over the bracelet before taking a step back to give her more breathing room.

"What am I looking for?" she asked, her fingers running over the white gold chain and charms.

"I'm not sure. *Something.*" I put a hand on my hip and chewed the thumb nail on my opposite hand. "Could there be a tracking device in one of the charms?"

She shook her head. "Any sort of transmission not cleared by the duke would have flagged the system. There's signal-blocking sheeting in the walls, so everything is filtered through the repeater first."

Explosives maybe?"

"Explosives?" the werewolf tech asked under his breath as he joined us. "Let me see that." He took the bracelet from the half-sired and held it up under his nose, sniffing loudly before handing it to me. "Nope. Just a bit of blood and perfume." He blew out a relieved sigh.

"Blood?" I lifted an eyebrow.

"Yeah." He shrugged. "Not so surprising in a house full of vamps, though."

I turned the bracelet over and inspected the charms and then the clasp, flicking it open to reveal a small bit of dried blood under the curl of the fastening hooks on the underside. They looked about the same distance apart as the scratches I'd seen on Yoshiko's arm.

"What are you doing down here?" Murphy asked, stepping out of his office behind me. I jumped and spun around, red flooding my vision again.

"I just had a question…for the tech team." I closed my hand around Polly's bracelet, trying to hide it from him.

Murphy's nostrils flared, and then he snatched my wrist as his pupils dilated. "Why do I smell Yoshiko's blood on you?"

I swallowed, unable to come up with a satisfactory answer that wasn't a lie. I couldn't let him know what I'd just learned. He'd slaughter the girl before we had a chance to question her.

"Murphy—" I pleaded as he took hold of my fingers and pried them open.

"Is that…?" He stared down at the bracelet in my palm, his fangs pushing out his upper lip. "Does that belong to the duke's new pet?" he asked, voice raw with quiet rage.

"No."

"But the crowns…" He fingered one of the dangling charms. Tears wet the corners of his eyes, and then he snatched up the bracelet and threw it to the floor, stomping his heel down on the delicate piece. "I'll kill her for this," he rasped before tearing off down the hall.

"Murphy, it's not hers!"

He turned and disappeared around the corner, heading up the stairs to the foyer. I chased after him. Several of the guards from the control room had heard the exchange and were close on my heels, but we were too far behind.

"Stop him!" I yelled up the stairwell, hoping the guards watching Dante's office doors would hear.

Shouts echoed through the foyer as I topped the stairs, and I found one of the guards slumped against a bench near the front entrance. The other clutched his shoulder, standing in the open doorway of the duke's office.

"What is the meaning of this?" Dante shouted over the man's shoulder, outraged that he was being prevented from leaving the safety of the room.

"Apologies, Your Grace," the guard blocking him said before unclipping the radio on his hip and pressing the call button. "We have a situation. All free guards, report to the south wing."

I rushed past him while he was distracted, narrowly missing the arm he threw out to stop me.

"Jenna!" Dante called from his office. "What is it?"

"Murphy! He's after Audrey," I shouted over my shoulder, picking up speed as I rounded the corner. I would have a harder time dodging Lane and the other guard on the south stairs.

Unless they abandon their posts to pursue Murphy, I thought upon seeing the empty stairwell.

"Murphy!" Lane shouted from farther up the hall. I spotted his partner, standing in Audrey's doorway, gaping helplessly after his boss. I pushed past him before he could think to stop me.

Inside the room, Lane had Murphy pinned in a half-Nelson over Audrey's bed. The girls cowered against the far wall, squealing in terror every time Murphy struggled to break free. The new donor-in-waiting stood in front of them, his legs spread and arms raised, ready to take on the vamp should Murphy get loose.

"She's the duke's future scion! What's wrong with you?" Levi growled. His eyes glowed yellow, and I saw the tips of his fingernails begin to curl.

He'd only just arrived at the manor, only just met the future baroness, but he was ready to faceoff with a vampire twice his size who was clearly out of his mind. All to protect Audrey and Polly.

Levi was a keeper. I mentally patted myself on the back for that one, even as I edged around the room to get to the girls. They both reached for me as I neared them, huddled together on the floor.

"Jenna!" Audrey rasped. "Thank *God*."

I pulled away from her and went for Polly, taking the girl's arms and dragging her up onto her feet.

"You can't be trusted near her," I said as she groped for Audrey, sensing my fury. "I'm taking you to the duke, right away."

Polly sucked in a shuddering breath. Her legs wobbled, and she slumped against me as she burst into tears. "It was an accident! I'm so sorry," she wailed.

"You?" Murphy snarled from the bed, struggling against Lane. Several more guards filed into the room and piled on top of him. "You're dead. Do you hear me? I'll drain you dry!" he shouted above their commands to calm down.

Polly's wailing turned into a shriek, and it was all I could do to hold her upright.

"What's this about?" Audrey snatched my arm and gaped up at me, her desperate eyes more pathetic than I could bear. "Can I come with you? *Please?*"

"Fine." I hated how callous I sounded, but I was unable to muster up a more sympathetic tone while holding the one responsible for ending Yoshiko's life. "We need to go. *Now.*"

Dante's office could be a scary place. I remembered my first visit, the nerves that had made every breath feel like razors in my lungs. And I hadn't even been in trouble. I could only imagine how someone as weak-willed and wretched as Polly must feel.

I stood behind Dante's desk, leaning against the wall with my arms folded over my chest, while the duke spoke with Audrey out in the foyer. I could understand why he wouldn't want her to see this side of him just yet, why he wouldn't want to alarm her with the uglier truths about House Lilith.

Polly shook uncontrollably, her sobs echoing inside the cup of her hands. I forced myself not to comfort her, remembering Scarlett's gift for conjuring sympathy. Her hasty apology was all the admission of guilt I needed—and everyone in Audrey's room had heard it. A seasoned spy, the girl was not.

Though...I couldn't quite believe that she was a coldhearted killer either. She'd been heavily supervised at Darkly Hall for the past eight years alongside Audrey and Kate.

One of the double doors opened, and Dante entered the office. He'd taken longer than I'd expected, but the broken bracelet in his hand explained why. He crossed the room and handed it to me with a humbled frown.

"Forgive my doubt, Your Grace," he said softly, his hand lingering on mine.

I looked down at the mangled chain and cracked charms,

pausing on one of the tiny coffins. It had been split open by Murphy's heel, revealing broken bits of plastic and wires.

"My harem manager's blood was found on your bracelet, Ms. Hughes," Dante said, taking a seat behind his desk. "Would you care to explain?"

"I'm so sorry." Polly's voice trembled. She'd repeated the apology a dozen times since I'd dragged her from Audrey's room. "It was an accident. I didn't mean to—"

"Didn't mean to what?" I snapped. "What exactly *were* you trying to do when you pushed her down the stairs?"

"She...she wouldn't give my bracelet back." Polly sniffled. "All I wanted was my bracelet."

"The bracelet you have been recording private conversations on around the manor, Ms. Hughes?" Dante clicked his tongue and folded his hands over the desk. "How uncivilized of you. What do you suppose Madam Madeira at Darkly Hall will have to say about your behavior?"

"I...I don't...I didn't..." Polly stammered, clearly distressed by how much we'd discovered.

"Who gave you the bracelet?" I asked, dangling it in front of her. Polly's eyes widened when she noticed the exposed charm.

"No. No! You have to fix it." She grasped for the bracelet, but I held it out of her reach. "They'll kill her! They'll kill Audrey just like they killed that girl from Bathory House."

"Who?" Dante demanded. His face was hard, and a noticeable bulge on either side of his mouth told me that he was running out of patience. "*Who?*" he repeated, louder.

"I don't know their names," Polly sobbed. "They just killed that girl in front of me and then gave me the bracelet. They told me to call Blood Vice to come get us."

"What else did they tell you?" I asked, shaking the bracelet at her. "We're not stupid. There's no transmitter on this. How did they expect to retrieve it from you?"

"One of them is going to be at the All Hallows' Eve ball." Polly dragged her hands down her face. "I'm supposed to give him the bracelet then. He said he'd leave Audrey alone after. But he said I had to put the bracelet in places around the house where it was most likely to record something worthwhile."

"Does this mean that you got a better look at your captors than was initially noted in the Blood Vice report?" Dante asked, struggling to speak around his extended fangs.

Polly sniffled. "If I did, can you stop them? Before they hurt Audrey?"

Dante looked up at me, a clear question in his eyes. This changed everything. I nodded slowly, understanding the advantage we now had. An opportunity like this wouldn't be dropped in our laps again anytime soon.

"The duchess is going to fetch her sketchpad," Dante told

Polly. "And when she returns, you will tell her *exactly* what your captors looked like."

"And you'll keep Audrey safe?" Polly asked, a hopeful pitch in her voice.

"As if you are truly concerned for her safety," Dante scoffed. "You intended to provide our enemies with intel on the innerworkings of this house—of Audrey's house. Did you really think that would contribute to her wellbeing?"

"The future baroness's safety is not in question." I stared at Polly, wondering if she had any sense of self-preservation or if her only concern was for her mistress. "But if it were"— I added, using the bait for encouragement— "you would do well to follow the duke's precise instructions."

"I will," Polly rasped. "I swear, I will. I'll make this right."

"You can't make what happened to Yoshiko right," I said, tossing the bracelet in Polly's face. "She figured you out, and you killed her for it. I'm sure Murphy wishes we'd do the same to you in return."

Polly gulped softly and then looked down at the mangled bracelet in her hands. "I didn't mean to. It really was an accident."

"But betraying us was not," Dante said. His tone had shifted. He was still angry, but I could tell he believed her— at least about Yoshiko. "Help us end this threat, and I will see to it that you are given a merciful end."

My heart stuttered at the thought of executing the girl. I was angry, too. Furious even. But were we really going to *kill* her? Was that the right thing to do? Would Murphy really demand such a thing once he had a chance to calm down?

Polly glanced up at us, her lashes thick with tears. "Tell me what to do."

Chapter Eighteen

A week's worth of plotting and scheming was not nearly enough—especially considering how long it took to get Murphy and Ursula on the same page with Dante and me— but a week was all the time we had to prepare before the queen's All Hallows' Eve ball.

The sketches I'd rendered with Polly's cooperation hadn't turned up anything useful, but after she'd detailed how strong the man in charge had been, and how pale his eyes were, it was clear that we had a half-sired suspect on our hands. I wondered if Kassandra deprived him intentionally for motivation. If he was going to be at the ball, he was probably a member of her harem.

Since the donors were not mentioned by name on the guest list, Dante easily swapped ours out with wolves from the guard. Levi was among them, determined to keep Audrey safe. She and Polly were the only humans in our party when we exited the jet in Denver Wednesday night, dressed in all the finery Ursula had coordinated for us.

One of the girls in the duke's harem who worked with jewelry repaired Polly's bracelet the best that she could. From a distance, it looked good as new. The charms dangled from her wrist in plain sight. The recording bits had even been repaired to keep up appearances, though the memory chip had been replaced with a new one that Dante had the tech team load with the score from *The Nutcracker*, the last ballet Kassandra had performed as a human—one that she'd badly botched.

Nerves chewed at my stomach, but I forced a smile at Audrey as we crossed the airport parking lot, prompting her to work on her own expression. We didn't have the advantage of a theater background like Kassandra. The ol' smile-and-nod routine would have to do.

Dante squeezed my hand. "This is it," he whispered, brushing a kiss on my cheek. Then we parted ways and loaded into the vehicles House McCoy had loaned us.

Ursula, Murphy, Mandy, and I rode in silence to the queen's estate. The quiet stilled my mind. This was the calm before the storm. A thoughtful meditation to prelude a party no one would soon forget.

The ball had already begun by the time we arrived, though we were still earlier than the prince and Kassandra.

"Her Highness, the Princess, and Her Grace, the Duchess Tempus of House Lilith," the doorman announced as he welcomed us inside the foyer of the queen's mansion.

A few dozen faces turned to watch us make our entrance.

Ursula gave them a smug smile and touched my back as she leaned into me, bringing her lips closer to my ear than necessary.

"These heathens are all asking themselves if we're lovers right now," she whispered, wrapping her fingers around the cap of my shoulder. "Which is probably less scandalous than the idea of you bedding the duke."

"I already told you that I'm not sleeping with Dante," I whispered through my teeth as I smiled at the gawking crowd.

"You and I both know that it's only a matter of time."

"Focus, Your Highness." I turned and batted my lashes at her, loosing a small giggle as if she'd said something amusing. "At least for the next hour. Then, you can go back to being your majestic, eccentric self."

Her smile faltered, but she quickly pasted it back on. "Give it time, sweetheart. No one lives through this much and comes out whole in the end."

I didn't have a reply for that, but I didn't need one. Lord McCoy greeted the princess. I split off from her to move deeper into the ballroom, searching every face I encountered for a freckle under the right eye, a pronounced cupid's bow, an angular chin.

I spotted Murphy in one of the side halls, his eyes crawling over the guests there. Mandy would be doing the same in the passages that led to the guest rooms and harem quarters. Just in case Kassandra had sent her minion to scope out the party ahead of her. In case he had somehow slipped in on the coattails of an accomplice that we were unaware of.

Once Murphy and the other guards who had come in behind us cleared the queen's mansion, they'd fetch Dante and the Darkly girls to set the snare. It was a careful plan, but there was always room for error. We had to be vigilant.

On my second pass through the ballroom, I bumped into Blair Hanson from my training unit at the bat cave.

"Your Grace," she said, inclining her head respectfully.

"Agent Hanson. Looking good." I nodded at her golden era dress, complete with feather boa and gloves.

"Says the vamp wearing a custom Vionnet." The laugh she followed the comment with was good-natured if a little envious. "I've been begging my sire for a Novak original," she confessed, her gloved hand held to the side of her mouth. "Maybe this Midwinter if I'm a good girl."

"If we make it this year, I'll look for you," I said, excusing myself as Kai Natani entered the foyer.

I wove through the crowd, but it had grown thicker as more guests arrived, and the task wasn't as easy as it had been before. I lost sight of the BATC instructor and found myself in the middle of the ballroom, spinning in a wide circle until my frustration gave way to panic.

Something sharp opened within me, a sensation I hadn't

felt for some time—one I didn't expect to feel ever again.

Maybe lifeblood bonds faded over time—but not *that* much time had passed. And Roman and I had shared *a lot* of blood. I knew the second he walked through the door, and every hair on my body rose. My heart trembled, praying for a merciful end.

His icy blues had already found me before I turned around. When our gazes clashed, I couldn't breathe. He stood in the mouth of the foyer, so perfectly still that I wondered if he were real. His white hair was cut shorter than I remembered, in a military cut, but he still wore a tux better than *007*.

Our intense stare across the room was interrupted when Vanessa appeared behind him. Her gown was a sophisticated, goth masterpiece, all black leather and tulle. She moved like a swan, her stoic gaze scanning the crowd. I turned away before she noticed me and headed for the nearest hallway. I didn't realize until I'd reached the mouth of it that it was the one leading to the art gallery where Roman and I had first caved to our lifeblood bond.

Not wanting to brave the ballroom again, I slipped deeper into the hall, moving toward the alcove that featured the vampire bust with the ruby fangs. It was an incredible sculpture—though, maybe not *quite* as incredible as I planned on pretending it was until I worked up the nerve to risk a run-in with Vanessa.

Now was not the time to hide out. I needed to be in the ballroom when Kassandra arrived.

I paced in front of the bust, folding and unfolding my arms, unable to stand still in my panic. Laughter bubbled and echoed down the hallway as the guests packed in tighter, some lingering in the arched opening to the ballroom. I moved farther down the hall, stopping just shy of the gallery door.

Go in, Roman's voice whispered in the back of my mind.

He hadn't opened the bond or spoke to me through it for so long that I had to wonder if I had imagined it. But then his very real hand wrapped around my waist. He pushed open the gallery door and pulled me in after him.

Before I could say a word, his mouth covered mine, his lips forcing mine open as he crushed me against the same wall we'd defiled a year ago. My blood boiled at his touch, his rough hands roaming my back above the corset that was suddenly too tight. I couldn't breathe.

"Roman," I finally rasped, wedging my arms between us. "We can't do this."

"We can," he insisted, his mouth reaching for mine again. "It's the only time we can do this."

"What?" My breath heaved in and out as I tried to comprehend what he was saying. "What are you talking about?"

"Tonight," he whispered, his fingers tangling in the laces that held my corset in place. "All Hallows' Eve—it's the only party of the queen's that the BATC facility is expected to attend."

"That's it?" I closed my eyes and held back an angry sob. "You think that's how we're going to make this work? An annual booty call?"

Roman sighed and tucked his face into the nook between my neck and shoulder, laying a wet kiss on my skin. "We have forever sprawled out before us. We don't need to have all the answers today."

The words had comforted me before. When he said them the last time we spoke, right before hanging up on me, they had broken my heart. Now, they just pissed me off.

"Get off me," I said, shoving at him.

He held me against the wall and tried to subdue me with another kiss, but I tilted my face away, forcing him to settle for my neck again. My breath labored as I writhed in his grasp, but Roman was a vampire now. A strong vampire who had been training new recruits at the bat cave all year.

Tears stung my eyes, and the dim gallery lit up red at my mounting panic, revealing the firm line of Roman's neck. It was so close. So inviting. My fangs elongated instinctively, and before I knew what I was doing, I struck.

Roman's breath hissed, and he went rigid against me. His

hands slapped on the wall to either side of my head as I drank from him.

His blood wasn't the same, though I hadn't expected it to be. I just thought...maybe...it would somehow make things right between us. Instead, it made everything so very wrong.

The Eye of Blood retraced his steps back to the last time Vanessa had anointed him as a human. She was angry, standing in the middle of a bedroom in a black bra and panties. Tears ran down her face, and then her hand lashed out, and I felt my head jerk to one side, felt my cheek burn from her touch.

"I'm sorry," I said with Roman's voice. Then my hands were on Vanessa, touching her face and her hip. My mouth met hers, lips catching on her fangs. Her tongue slid inside my mouth, lapping at the trickle of blood.

I didn't want to see any more, but I couldn't stop the vision no matter how hard I tried. Once the eye was triggered, it had to run its course. And every second of it destroyed me.

As soon as it ended, and I was back in my own skin, I released Roman. My fangs retracted, and I covered my mouth, panting.

Roman touched the side of his neck with the palm of one hand, then pulled it away to gauge the damage. The holes were already sealing, but two faded marks remained, smeared with his spoiled blood.

"What did you see?" he asked.

I lowered my hands from my mouth and swallowed. "Enough."

"It didn't mean anything," he said, reaching for me again. I pushed away from the wall and headed for the door. I couldn't be here anymore. I couldn't look at his face or this room for one more second. And I never, *never* wanted his blood in my mouth again.

"Jenna." Roman's hand squeezed around my arm, but I jerked it free and wrenched the door open.

"Your Grace," Vanessa greeted me with an unsurprised sneer. She glanced over my shoulder to where Roman stood, suddenly more interested in the toes of his shoes than me. Vanessa's eyebrows arched as she noticed the marks on his neck.

"I was just leaving," I said, trying to step around her.

"Still putting your fangs where they don't belong I see." She smirked at my guilty wince. "Don't worry, green fang. In fact, drink up." She cocked her head at Roman. "You'll forgive me if his nectar isn't as sweet or satisfying as you remember. Seems I had the last of his living blood before you went and got him killed."

"I have somewhere to be," I said, trying again to escape the gallery.

"Oh, pardon me, Your Grace," Vanessa said, sweeping

the tulle skirt of her dress back in a disdainful bow so I could pass.

I fled down the hallway, eager to find Mandy. I needed a hug from someone I could count on, from someone I could believe cared about me. As I spilled into the ballroom, it was Dante I ran into first.

"Ms. Skye." He took in my face with startled surprise and immediately pulled a handkerchief from the pocket of his suit. "Let me," he said as I reached for it.

"Where's Audrey?" I asked, glancing around the room.

"With Ursula and Mandy. She's perfectly fine." Dante turned me toward one of the outer walls, hiding my face from the bulk of the crowd as he ran the silk cloth under my eyes and over the corners of my mouth where I suspected there was smeared lipstick and dried blood. His eyebrows arched sullenly at the evidence.

"I ran into Roman," I said, unable to bring myself to lie to him. "And now I wish you hadn't killed him so I could have tonight."

"Did he harm you?" Dante asked, the sorrow in his expression melting into wrath.

"No more than I harmed him." I blushed and took the handkerchief from Dante, rubbing it more vigorously at my mouth. "Any sign of our special guest?"

Before he could answer, the doorman shouted over the

din of the crowd.

"His Highness, the Prince, and Her Grace, the Duchess of House Lilith."

I tucked the handkerchief back into Dante's pocket and tried to fluff it the way Ursula had at the manor before we left. It was useless, but the duke didn't try to fix it when I was done. He was too distracted by the hand signal Murphy was giving him from across the room.

"Showtime," I said, taking the arm Dante extended to me.

Chapter Nineteen

Kassandra painted an elegant, innocent picture in the mouth of the foyer. She wore a high-waisted, Jane Austen-esque gown, her dark curls secured with a satin ribbon. Her Mr. Darcy, the prince, stepped in beside her, holding out his arm for her to take. They turned and stared across the room at Dante and me, our postures eerily mirroring theirs.

I felt Dante's arm tense under my hand. "He will not like this," Dante said.

"But it has to be done." I smiled weakly as the prince nodded at us. "You're not having doubts, are you?" I whispered.

Dante pressed his lips together and tilted his head closer to mine. "If ever there were a worse time for doubt, I cannot fathom it."

"Agreed." I dipped into a proper curtsey as the prince and Kassandra stopped in front of us. "Your Highness, Your Grace," I greeted them.

Kassandra gave me an odd smile, and I realized she was trying very hard to mask her scorn. I'd upset her plans to get rid of Ursula—more than once.

"Happy All Hallows' Eve, brother," Kassandra said to Dante. "I was hoping to meet your future baroness tonight. Lili failed to mention that you were bringing the duchess tempus instead." She gave me another smile that wasn't a smile at all, but I returned the expression the best I could.

"Oh, Audrey is here. The princess, as well. Somewhere," Dante said, waving a casual hand out at the crowd. "She accompanied my pending scion to the powder room. You know how ladies can be." He tossed a wry smile at Alexander.

The prince laughed and touched Dante's shoulder affectionately. "We are eager to meet your chosen. You will make an exceptional sire."

"You flatter me." Dante blushed, and I suspected the praise had further wounded his resolve. Alexander was the one hiccup that could ruin our plans tonight.

Kassandra pulled gently at the prince's arm. "If you'll excuse us, we must pay our respects to the dear queen before the new Blood Vice recruits line up for their turn."

"We were just on our way to do the same," Dante said, the good cheer fading somewhat from his voice. "After you, sister," he added, opening his hand to the side.

Alexander smiled again and then let Kassandra tug him through the crowd. Every head along the way dipped with respect as the guests parted for our regal parade.

Right before we reached the doors to the throne room, Ursula and Audrey appeared.

"Cousin," Ursula offered the prince her hand. He gave her a tight smile but followed through with the proper greeting and kissed her knuckles.

"We missed you at Midsummer," Kassandra said to the princess, dropping the mandatory inch to show her respect.

"Of course you did, poor dear." Ursula gave the duchess a pitying smile. "Well, don't you worry. I'll be at every ball from here on out."

Kassandra's fake smile didn't fail her, but a tendon in her neck bulged, straining against her pale flesh. "Wonderful," she said breathlessly, green eyes smoldering.

I traded spots with Audrey, releasing Dante's arm so she could take it. Tonight, before the queen, my place was at Ursula's side.

Kassandra's attention fell briefly to our matching outfits, and her eyes widened with some awareness that I didn't grasp until we entered the throne room. Ursula's green and black theme was reflected in the décor, and then I realized it wasn't her color scheme at all—or, at least, the princess's scheme had nothing to do with party colors.

The queen sat on her throne, elevated on a dais in the back corner of the room. Her elaborate gown was clearly another Vionnet creation, also done in the green and black that everyone was dressed in—everyone besides the prince and Kassandra.

I had to admire Ursula's ability to keep this little nugget of pettiness under wraps all this time. It didn't change anything in the plan, but any surprise, no matter how small, disrupted the calm I was desperately clinging to. I gave Ursula a wide-eyed glare that she ignored as she greeted the queen.

"You look lovely, Your Majesty."

Lili's sharp gaze took us in, lingering longer on the prince and duchess before drawing back to Ursula. She didn't say anything, but the knowing look on her face suggested that she was onto the princess's biting game.

"Is this the one?" Lili asked. She stood and walked down the steps of the platform. As she neared, everyone dropped into the proper bow or curtsey, including me. Ursula's lessons were paying off. Although, the nerves eating me alive stunted my pride.

Dante led his prospective scion forward by the hand. "I give you Audrey Anne Moore of Darkly Hall," he said.

The queen hummed to herself, and then her thumb and forefinger snatched Audrey's chin, drawing a soft gasp from the girl.

"Open," Lili demanded. Audrey obeyed instantly, and the queen leaned in closer to examine her teeth, testing a finger to the underside of each canine. "You'll have a strong, clean bite when you're reborn."

"Thank you, Your Majesty," Audrey said, curtseying a second time as soon as the queen released her face.

Lili fingered one of Audrey's strawberry curls next, and a

shadow of a smile touched her mouth. "Darkly does love their redheads," the queen mused. "A tribute to Lilith's eternal beauty, I presume."

The vision I'd had the night Lili anointed me was my only glimpse of the ancient queen, but it was memorable. With Lili's comment, I could see the resemblance now. Audrey was a younger, innocent version of Lilith.

"My lovely sire," Alexander said as the queen stopped in front of him. He kissed her hand, and I watched as the tendon in Kassandra's neck flexed. Lili seemed to notice, too.

"Now that your firstborn has found a suitable human to sire," the queen said, "I expect your second to begin interviewing potentials, too."

Alexander swallowed, and his brows drew together somberly, reminding me a bit of Dante. "As you wish, Your Majesty."

The doors to the throne room opened suddenly, and the roar of the party filtered inside as the duke's guards dragged a man before the queen. Murphy and Donnie held the man's arms behind his back and forced him to his knees. I noted the freckle under his right eye, the pronounced cupid's bow and angular chin. He looked just like the sketch—though his eyes were a dark brown.

Dante waited until the throne room doors had closed again. Then he said, "I believe the duchess began interviewing prospects some time ago." The corners of his eyes drooped as he looked at Alexander. "I regret how this had to be done. Forgive me, sire. But it is better to seek mercy from the queen than undergo a public spectacle from the council."

Lili watched silently, waiting for the punchline with a mildly annoyed look on her face.

"Phillip?" the prince said, looking down at the restrained man. "What is the meaning of this?"

Kassandra's breath heaved violently. She glanced back at the double doors as if she were ready to bolt, but the prince took her hand in both of his. His eyes consumed her, begging for an explanation—for an answer that would refute Dante's claim.

"Don't look at me like that," Kassandra hissed. "It's a lie, of course. Your precious duke has never liked me."

Dante stepped in closer to the man—Phillip—and placed a hand on top of his head, tilting it back so his dark eyes stared up at Dante. A faint ring around the man's brown irises revealed how he was hiding his half-sired status. Dante ran a thumb over the surface of one of the man's eyes, rubbing the contact free and revealing the pale gray iris beneath.

"*Kassandra*," the prince scolded. She ripped her hand out of his and turned to snarl at Dante, her fangs budding beneath the curl of her upper lip. "You're a liar! You anointed him yourself so you could ruin me. Tell them, Phillip!"

Phillip's mismatched eyes glared up at her, but he obeyed. "I am a spy of the duke's," he said with resentful conviction.

"Would I hire a spy to slaughter my potential scions?" Dante asked. "We have a witness who saw you take the life of Ingrid Kelley, the potential scion I chose from Bathory House—the same witness you tried to blackmail into bugging my home in Ladue." Dante's stare rose to meet Kassandra's. "You had them murdered until you found one weak-willed enough to do your bidding."

"Lies! All lies!" Kassandra cried, balling her fists. "The only thing I am guilty of is trusting one of your snakes in my garden." She glared down at Phillip. Her contempt was raw and honest, but I imagined it had more to do with the fact that he'd been caught—that *she'd* been caught.

Dante gave Kassandra a pitying frown. "I am still one step ahead of you, sister."

Another door on the opposite side of the room opened. Two of the queen's guards entered the room, pushing in a pair of coffins on wheeled carts. A costumed servant followed them with a tray containing the queen's ceremonial dagger. It had been polished and prepared for the initiation of the new Blood Vice agents, but Dante had other plans for it first.

Phillip's shoulders slumped at the sight of the coffins. He knew his name was on one of them, that it was his only ride out of this room. Dante put a hand on Phillip's head again, but this time, he wrapped his other hand under the man's angular chin.

"No," Kassandra gasped. "You can't!"

I held my breath, knowing what came next. One sharp twist and a grinding snap, and Phillip went limp in Murphy's and Donnie's arms. His head lolled to one side, a blue vein showing through his transparent flesh.

Dante waved a hand at the servant carrying the queen's dagger, beckoning him to come closer. "We need not argue. The truth is in the blood. Your fate is in the queen's hands now," he said, taking the blade from the tray. He dragged it across the side of Phillip's neck, coating its sharp edge with the man's blood.

Dante laid the dagger back on the tray, and the servant offered it to the queen with a dramatic bow. The formalities around here were so tedious, I found myself longing for the casual comfort of the manor.

Lili picked up the dagger, giving each of us a disappointed scowl before licking the blood from the blade. I knew how awkward and intense the visions could be. The idea of suffering through one in front of such a crowd unnerved me. The queen couldn't have been happy about it either.

Her eyelids flickered, and she stared blankly over the room, seeing things that were somewhere else, trapped in another time. We watched her with bated breath—all except for Kassandra. The duchess turned and made for the double doors we'd entered through, slipping past the duke's guards while they were distracted.

Alexander spun around, ready to give chase, but Dante grabbed the prince's arm, holding him back. The visions never lasted long, though they could feel like forever. The queen's dagger zipped through the air, right past Alexander's devastated face. The blade caught Kassandra between the shoulder blades, and she went down with a wounded shriek.

"Kassandra!" the prince cried. His fangs elongated, and his eyes filled with black as he broke free of Dante's hold with a snarl. "Look what you've done!"

"Alexander." The queen's back straightened, and she folded her hands under her breasts, the epitome of wrathful serenity. "Wait for me in my bedchamber," she ordered him.

He looked across the room to where the duchess sat slumped on the floor, the queen's dagger still protruding from her back, blood slowly staining her dress. "But Kassandra—"

"—will be dealt with," the queen finished, her gaze sliding to the two coffins. "Along with her illegitimate pet."

"She is my scion," Alexander pleaded. "Let me exact her punishment."

"I am your queen," Lili said, her voice hardening. "You will do as I command."

Alexander bowed his head. "Yes, Your Majesty." His gaze

migrated to Kassandra again as if he knew it would be some time before he next laid eyes on her. But the hopelessness gave way to resentment as he looked back at Dante and me.

There was a promise in the prince's eyes, one we couldn't give back. We may have thwarted one enemy, but we'd made another in the process.

Chapter Twenty

The look on Alexander's face was still burned in my mind. He blamed this on me. In some ways, I supposed it was my fault. But more than that, I felt the threat stirring within him, the eye-for-an-eye conclusion that Dante's betrayal had inspired.

"Put them in the coffins," Lili commanded, nodding to the duchess and Phillip. The half-sired minion was unconscious, and he would be for a few more hours. Transferring him to the first coffin was easy, and two of Dante's guards took the task upon themselves, leaving the queen's guards to tend to the duchess.

"My queen, grandsire," Kassandra sobbed. "Have mercy."

"The coffins are lined with velvet, treacherous girl," the queen replied. "That is all the mercy I have left for you."

Kassandra yelped as a guard yanked the dagger out of her back, and her blood flowed more freely down the folds of her dress. It pooled on the floor behind her. The queen's manservant hurried across the room, and the guard placed the dagger on the tray, the blade dripping thick blood over the shiny surface. Then the guards each took up one of the duchess's arms and dragged her backward, leaving a blood trail on the floor that her gown smeared through.

As they hauled her past Dante, she kicked and screamed at him. Her lips peeled back, revealing swollen gums and extended fangs. She hissed and thrashed like a wild animal.

"This isn't over!" she screamed. "You think you've won? This is only the beginning. A coffin will not hold me forever."

"Rest in peace, sister," Dante said as the guards lifted Kassandra into the second box. Panic filled her eyes as they began to close the top, and one last scream unfurled from her throat, sending goosebumps along my skin. Then, it was snuffed out, muffled as the lid clicked shut.

Audrey sniffled beside me, and I realized how alarming all of this must be for her. I wasn't exactly used to it myself. I wrapped my arm around her and pulled her in close, hoping tonight wouldn't motivate her to follow Kate back to Austin.

I didn't have to like her, but I could at least play nice. If I didn't, I feared these older vamps would be us one day, stabbing each other in the back over a crown that anyone with a lick of sense wouldn't want anyway.

"You will go home," the queen said, turning her back to us. "Tonight, after we are done here. I will anoint the new warriors and retire for the evening. The guards and servants can handle the rest of the party."

"And Alexander?" Dante asked, placing a hand over his heart.

"Alexander is not your problem." The queen sighed and

finally turned around. "Of all my children, how did you turn out to be the most loyal and trustworthy?"

When Dante didn't answer, the queen sniffed and looked at Ursula, standing beside me with her hands folded in front of her fancy dress and an unreadable expression on her face. The princess had surprisingly kept it together throughout the events of the night.

Dante's remark about Ursula acting out so boldly to get it out of her system came back to me. Maybe she did just need someone at home who understood her insecurities and tolerated her quirks the way Morgan had, so she could function again among the undead without going stark-raving mad.

Sometimes, the people we loved kept us grounded, and when they left this world, they took a tiny piece of our sanity with them—or maybe a good chunk of it, in Ursula's case. I knew I'd lost a sliver of my rationality and reason with my mother's passing.

"You're going to be queen one day," Lili said, drawing the princess's undivided attention. "I will take Alexander to my forever rest, and you will be the third vampiric queen of House Lilith to rule over this territory. What kind of queen will you be, Ursula?"

The princess opened her mouth, but nothing came out. Whatever offense she'd taken, she kept it to herself. Her eyes welled as she pressed her lips together again. "I will do my very best, my queen."

"But will that be enough?" Lili sighed. "I have reigned for two hundred and thirty-three years. I am tired, but I fear handing this crown over to you will mean the end of House Lilith."

"Then take me with you and leave Alexander behind," Ursula begged. "I am ready."

Lili shook her head. "I will honor the blood oath I made to my scion, and this burden will be yours, whether you want it or not."

"Then—" Ursula panted and looked up at me as if suddenly realizing that she'd just volunteered to leave her vampling scion high and dry. I was surprised by how slighted I felt. "Then give the crown to Dante."

"Leave." The queen turned her back again, tiring of arguing with the princess. "Go back to St. Louis. We will speak more of this at Imbolc. I do not wish to see you again until then. Let Midwinter pass with your peaceful absence."

I hadn't expected the queen to do cartwheels over Kassandra's betrayal, but a little gratitude for finally evicting the rotten apple from her cart would have been nice. Still, I didn't express my disappointment as the duke led us from the throne room.

Lane and Mandy waited with the rest of the guards in a

cluster around Polly. The queen hadn't asked for any specifics about the donor-in-waiting who had been blackmailed. After four hundred years, I imagined she viewed most humans as lapdogs—harmless, adoring pets with stunted lifespans. But every now and then, one needed to be put down.

I wondered what would become of Philip. As a new vampire, if he didn't receive blood within the first few days, he would become a ravenous creature with no chance of revival. He was as good as dead. I wanted to believe it was justice, but who knew what Kassandra had bribed or threatened Phillip with to earn his allegiance. Vampires took extortion and intimidation to a whole new level.

Audrey left my side to go to Polly. The girls hugged, and I saw Murphy watching them with a scowl. Dante had promised Polly a merciful end for her cooperation in exposing Kassandra. Did Murphy know that? I wasn't sure what the duke had told him before we left the manor, but whatever it was, it had pacified Murphy for the time being.

"She will be returned to Austin," Dante said, coming to a stop beside me. He touched my shoulder, drawing my worried stare away from the girls. "It was Murphy's decision, though I made him wait three days before bringing it to me. He needed time to get his head right."

"You didn't tell the queen," I said, wondering where the line of justice fell for the duke. How was Phillip guilty and

Polly not?

"Polly tried to do the right thing," Dante said, a crease worrying his brow.

"*After* she was caught."

"She's just a girl," he added. "And she was coerced."

"You don't think Phillip was?" I asked.

Dante grinned softly. "I could give you access to the Blood Vice database, let you do some digging to see if there is a loved one somewhere that he was protecting."

"You could," I said, nodding.

I wasn't sure if Dante was serious or not, but I was up for the task. It wasn't like I had etiquette lessons to stay on top of for Midwinter. Guess Blair would have to show off her dress to someone else.

Ursula slipped one arm around Dante's shoulders and the other around mine. "Well, children. One villain down, a few hundred to go."

I snorted. "All kinds of things are possible when we get out of the house."

She gave me a level look. "I wonder what was possible when you two ran off to Chicago. Thought you were keeping secrets, did you?" she said at my surprise.

"You're one to talk," I snapped back at her. "Matching our dresses and suits to the queen's throne room."

"What?" She blinked innocently. "I assumed Kassandra

would have found out about the color palette through one of her spies. It's not my fault that Vionnet was all booked up before she got around to asking him and was forced to settle for a Novak knockoff."

I gazed out over our small party, all dressed in custom, matching attire. "No, not your fault at all."

Dante cleared his throat as one of the guards signaled that the cars were ready. "The duchess and I have some things to discuss, cousin," he said to Ursula. "Would you mind accompanying my pending scion and her dowry donor to the airport?"

"Mm-hmm." She rolled her eyes and left us to join the others.

The night air was cool against my skin. I looked back at the queen's mansion, wondering if Roman and Vanessa were still inside or if they'd left after the incident in the gallery. I was anxious to leave before I ran into either of them again.

The first car pulled away with Ursula and the Darkly girls, and then Donnie pulled the second car ahead for Dante and me to load into. I didn't know what he wanted to talk to me about, but I hoped it was nothing dire. I'd had about enough of that for one night.

Donnie closed the back door and ran around the car to climb into the driver's seat. Then we pulled around and out of the drive, heading back toward the airport. Dante fiddled with a few dials, adjusting the heat and music, and then he hit the button for the partition that separated the front seats from the back.

Dante didn't wait for it to finish closing before he turned and cupped my face with both hands, pulling me in for a chaste kiss. He placed one on each cheek before going back to my mouth for seconds, his lips touching my skin as softly as a whispered breath.

"I almost lost myself tonight," he said, pausing to press his forehead to mine. "I would not have made it through without you by my side."

"Are you all right?" I asked. The kisses felt like victory, but I knew better. Alexander was not pleased. Angering Dante's sire hadn't been part of the plan, but we knew it was a potential risk.

Dante shrugged and gave me a sad smile. "One step forward, two steps back."

I leaned forward and pressed another kiss to his mouth, enjoying the tenderness of his touch, the slow way his fingers caressed my skin. A duchess could get used to this.

The desperate, taboo thrill of Roman had been…exhilarating. But it wasn't enough, and it never would be. And it certainly wasn't love. Whatever lustful longings remained from our blood bond, I was over them.

Dante kissed me again, his eyes open and searching mine. *Is this okay?* They seemed to ask. I answered by parting my lips the next time his met mine. His hand pressed firmly against the side of my corset, and I sighed shallowly as the bones of the garment dug into my skin.

"How can you breathe in such a contraption?" he asked, grinning as his hands slid around to my backside and he searched for a way to free me.

"We should wait," I whispered against his cheek. Ursula would kill me if I got anything on the gown she'd had commissioned, and I wasn't even sure how I'd get the thing off and on again in such a tight space.

"My dear lady." Dante gave me a horrified look. "I have no intention of bedding you in a moving vehicle—at least, not for our first time."

"Then what are you doing?" I rasped, enjoying the sensation of the corset loosening as his hands worked the laces in back.

"Brainstorming other...*pleasurable* things we can do to pass the time." His mouth dipped down to my collarbone, and I sighed more fully this time, my lungs no longer constricted. "Ah, that's better," he said, dragging his mouth back in the opposite direction.

I could already tell that the plane ride would be torture.

Maybe all kinds of things were possible when we got out of the house. But right now, I couldn't wait to get home.

Catch up with Jenna and company in…

FLESH AND BLOOD

BLOOD VICE BOOK SEVEN

Available Now!

After a year of playing scion to the temperamental Princess of House Lilith, Jenna is ready to get back to solving cases—even if that means sneaking out of the manor to get the job done. Jenna's antics do not go unnoticed by the Vampiric High Council. When several representatives drop in to conduct the princess and duchess's one-year evaluation and are nearly taken out by a poorly-timed bomb, the council decides to put Jenna's skills as an agent to the test. If she can uncover whoever is behind the attack, the council will approve her arrangement with the princess. Otherwise, there's a locked coffin in her immediate future—a future she's just learned could include a living niece or nephew.

ACKNOWLEDGMENTS

Thanks to all the usual peeps who help me make these books happen: Chelle Olson, my epic editor, who works so hard to make my words pretty (even when I miss deadlines—sorry!); Rebecca Frank, who designed another lovely cover; my cover model, a.k.a. little seester, who knows how to strike a pose; Hollie Jackson, who brings Jenna's voice to life in the audiobooks; my critique group, the Four Horsemen of the Bookocalypse, who are always supportive and inspiring; THE Professor George Shelley, for proofreading my books—even though I've strayed from Limbo City; my sweet son, who reminds me of the importance of taking a break every now and then to watch Tinker Bell and eat popcorn with him; my husband, who once again kept everything from going to hell in a handbasket while I panicked over fleeting deadlines; and all my Grim Readers, who take time to send encouraging emails, leave reviews, and hang out with me on online. You guys rock!

ABOUT THE AUTHOR

USA Today bestselling fantasy author **Angela Roquet** is a great big weirdo. She lives in Missouri with her husband and son in a house stuffed with books, toys, skulls, owls, and glitter-speckled craft supplies. She's a member of SFWA and HWA, as well as the Four Horsemen of the Bookocalypse, her epic book critique group, where she's known as Death. When not swearing at the keyboard, she enjoys boating with her family at Lake of the Ozarks and reading books that raise eyebrows. You can find Angela online at
www.angelaroquet.com

If you enjoyed this book, please leave a review.
Your support and feedback are greatly appreciated!

CPSIA information can be obtained
at www.ICGtesting.com
Printed in the USA
BVHW041656131022
649391BV00005B/205